THE SONG
OF THE
LOST BOY

ABOUT THE AUTHOR

Maggie Allder was born and brought up in Gamlingay in Cambridgeshire, the second daughter of a village police officer. She studied at King Alfred's College, Winchester (now the University of Winchester), in Richmond, Virginia, and later at Reading university, and taught for 36 years in a comprehensive school. After exploring and appreciating more orthodox forms of Christianity, Maggie became a Quaker, and is happy and settled in the Quaker community in Winchester. She has previously written three novels which form a trilogy: 'Courting Rendition, 'Living with the Leopard' and 'A Vision Softly Creeping.'Maggie volunteers for a not-for-profit organisation, Human Writes, which aims to provide friendship to prisoners on death row in the USA.

THE SONG OF THE LOST BOY

MAGGIE ALLDER

This is a work of fiction. Names, characters, businesses, places, events
and incidents are either the products of the author's imagination
or used in a fictitious manner. Any resemblance to actual persons,
living or dead, or actual events is purely coincidental.

Matador
9 Priory Business Park,
Wistow Road, Kibworth Beauchamp,
Leicestershire, LE8 0RX
Tel: 0116 279 2299
Email: books@troubador.co.uk
Web: www.troubador.co.uk/matador
Twitter: @matadorbooks

ISBN 978 1789015 638

British Library Cataloguing in Publication Data.
A catalogue record for this book is available from the British Library.

Printed and bound in Great Britain by 4edge Limited
Typeset in 11pt Aldine40 BT by Troubador Publishing Ltd, Leicester, UK

Matador is an imprint of Troubador Publishing Ltd

To everyone in Winchester Quaker Meeting, who together have created such a welcoming and challenging community.

CHAPTER 1

Home

There is an Old Man who lives on top of the Hill. *St Catherine's Hill,* they call it, although as far as I can tell, St Catherine has never done anything to lay claim to it. She does not send police or anti-terrorist people in riot gear, to defend her hill and to turf us off. Perhaps that is because she is a saint? When the People bring us food and water, the Old Man says that they must be saints. Saints do good to other people, but property is a crime, so how can Catherine be a saint and own a hill?

It seems to me as if the Hill belongs to the Old Man. Not *belongs* the way that cars belong to their drivers, so that if you break into them and drive away, or even just take a device from the dashboard, they can lock you up or put you in care (which is the same thing), but *belongs* like washing hanging on a line belongs to people. It is their clothes. When they are dry the people the clothes belong to will want to wear them again, and if you creep into their garden and take their clothes, for example, if you really like the colour or your own shorts have worn a hole in them, then what will the previous owners do? Wear their pyjamas to work? Or take clothes from someone else's line? The problem would go on forever that way.

I think that the Hill belongs to the Old Man because if someone were to take it away from him, where would he go? We usually live up there, and we sometimes live in the nature reserve, and sometimes in the winter we go north to Basingstoke and hide in an old warehouse, but only if we really have to, if it snows or is frosty for a long time, or if the police are after us. But the Old Man is always there. Skye said he is like a rock, and calls him Peter, because she says Peter was a rock. I do not know this Peter, the rock, but I like the colour of his name. In my head *Peter* is a bluish-green colour, a little bit shiny. *Catherine*, the owner of the Hill, has a name which is softly grey and beige, and maybe a little pink, a gentle name, but not a name that goes with the Hill. The Hill is quite high (but, Skye says, not as high as the hills in Wales, which she would like me to see sometime). It has a copse of trees on the top, and circular earthworks made a long time ago, before I was born, even before the Old Man was born. There is a sort of maze too, cut into the turf. *Turf* is one of the few words that looks the same colour in my head as it is in real life, pale green with a sort of straw colour mixed in. *Turf* is a word with lots of meanings. The first meaning is *territory*, like when a beggar in the High Street told me to scram, because that was his turf. The second meaning is, Skye says, a verb. A verb is a doing word, and Sky has been trying to teach us about them because, she says, everyone should know a little grammar. When *turf* is a doing word it means you get thrown out. They turfed us out of the multi-storey car park once, and we were lucky they did not lock the lot of us up, they said, and throw away the key. But *turf* also means a patch of grass, with the roots all knotted up together underneath and sometimes some daisy roots in the mix, and if you cut it carefully you can make a fire on the bare earth underneath, and when you move on you can put the turf back and it will grow into place again, and after a little while it will be hard to tell you were ever there.

The Hill is green which, as I pointed out earlier, is not the colour of *Catherine* in my head, so I sometimes wonder whether Catherine took the Hill from someone else. Who knows? Skye says the world is full of things we do not know, and from my experience I would say that seems true. I am trying to learn, though. We are all learning, all the kids. I heard Skye say so, to the Old Man. "They learn something new every day," she said, and the Old Man grunted, which means he is pleased.

I can count as high as anyone, but I cannot count the number of kids here, in our camp. For one thing, the numbers keep changing. People come and go, which is normal, and once a new baby came, with a lot of screaming and fuss. But there is another problem with trying to count the number of kids, and that is not knowing when a kid turns into an adult. *Kid* means *baby goat* and it does not have a strong colour in my head, but it also means a child who is not yet old enough to go to prison or into a labour camp. A kid goes into care, but Skye says they always end up in prison in the long run.

I am definitely still a kid. None of us knows how old I am because, somewhere along the line, I lost my mum and dad. I do not know how I did that, but I know I lost them, because I heard Skye tell some other adults one night, when we were sitting round the fire after drinking the hot soup the People brought (the people who are supposed to be saints), and I was almost asleep with my head on Skye's lap and my feet towards the warm, crackling fire.

"Is he your grandchild?" one of the adults had asked. Nobody would think I was Skye's son because she is an old lady with a long white plait down her back and a wrinkled face.

"No, he's not mine," said Skye, "although he feels like mine, sometimes. I just picked him up when he was scrounging outside a supermarket. It seems he has lost his parents."

I lost my favourite toy once. It was a little droid, a solar-powered thing with a cracked screen that I found down by the river. Skye said that I couldn't get the internet on it, but I do not really know about the internet so I did not mind. If I left it in the sun, though, and it powered up, I could play games on it. Then I took it with me, in the pocket of my shorts, when we went to the High Street one Wednesday night, when all the shops put out the rubbish and we go gleaning, and when I got back, my toy had gone. I must have dropped it. I wanted to go back and find it, but it was beginning to get light, and they collect the rubbish early, and Skye said I might be caught and, although she did not say so, we both knew that they might put me in care. Skye said, "You'd better just accept it's lost," and gave me a hug. It was easy to lose that toy, but how could I have lost my parents, two fully grown adults?

I have a feeling in my tummy, or maybe it is in my head, that I will try to find my lost parents. I would like to have a mum and a dad, like some of the other kids have.

★ ★ ★

I like it best when Skye is in the camp, and I like it best when we are on the Hill, not in the nature reserve or in a warehouse, so the very best times for me are in the summer, on the Hill, sitting round a fire on a night when they are not going to go gleaning, and we talk and sing songs. The evenings usually go like this: during the day the camp is quite empty. Mums who have got young babies or really little kids stay near the shelters, but everyone else goes off to do whatever it is they do. Usually I play with the other boys. My friends are Dylan, Big Bear and Little Bear (who are brothers), Storm and Limpy; but any other boys who happen to be in the camp can play with us too. We do not play with the girls because girls play different games. They usually make a camp in the trees and pretend to be mothers, or fairies, which to be honest seems pretty boring. We play *Police and Squatters.* Half of us are police and we carry sticks which we pretend are tasers, and the other half are squatters. The squatters make a shelter and lie down to go to sleep. The police hide behind one of the earthworks, and then at a particular signal they rush over the top of the bank and shout and point at the squatters. Then there is a fight. In real life, the squatters would always lose, but in our games it is fifty-fifty and that is because the tasers are only sticks and the squatters can pick up sticks too.

Usually, before the sun is right overhead (if there is any sun) someone calls us together to give us lessons. We are Scum of the Earth (I read that in a piece of newspaper) and so we are not allowed to go to real schools, but we do not care. We like our lessons, which anyone from the camp can give us, as long as the Old Man approves of what they plan to teach. We can learn myths and legends, but not religion, because religion is the cause of so much trouble. We learn letters and words, and now Skye is teaching us the basics of grammar, and we learn how numbers work. Numbers are a sort of magic. We learn about places and things that have happened long ago, before we were born. One summer when I was still really small a man taught us how to make pottery out of clay, but my pot collapsed in the fire so I have nothing to show for that, and the man went away and did not come back.

When the shadows get long everyone starts coming back up the Hill. Some go and talk to the Old Man about whatever has happened that day, others find their partners or their children and have drinks together, and people light, or stoke up, their fires ready for cooking. If she is there I always eat at Skye's fire, and usually there are quite a lot of other people sitting round too, because Skye is funny and kind. Sometimes she goes away. She used to want me to go with her but I want to stay here, on the Hill, because I think Winchester is the place where I lost my mum and dad, and I always have it in my mind that I might find them again. If Skye is away I usually hang around with Big Bear and Little Bear. They have a mum, and their mum has a bloke, who is not their dad, called Walking Tall.

5

Walking Tall is actually a short man, the same height as their mum, but Big Bear told me that he walks tall, which means he does not give in to other people, and has self-respect, and that is a good thing. I think maybe the Old Man gave him the name *Walking Tall* when he first came to us. Big Bear said his mum was very sad in those days, but she is happy now. Walking Tall used to carry me round on his shoulders when I was small but he says I am a big fella now and he is not strong enough. Last time Skye went away, Walking Tall built a bit extra onto their shelter, which is the one nearest to the trees, with the grassy roof. He said it was getting to be a tight squeeze now that we are all growing into such likely lads. It is fun in their shelter but I like Skye's better, and best of all I would like to live in a shelter with my own mum and dad.

★ ★ ★

I was very little when Skye found me, but not so little that I could not talk. Skye says I kept asking for my mummy, but there was nobody around in the supermarket car park who seemed to be a likely candidate, and the police were systematically searching the undergrowth where people sometimes hide. Skye told me that she went back every day for a week trying to find someone to claim me, but without success. It was the Old Man who told her that the best thing to do was to keep me with her. "I couldn't take you to Social Services myself," she explained, "I was a wanted person, and anyhow they would have put you in care. I couldn't live with myself…"

Care is the scariest thing for us kids at the camp. We tell each other endless stories about the things that go on in care, but sometimes I think that most of what we say is made up. Still, we can feel the adults' anxiety, and we know to stay well away from anyone in a uniform, or those sorts of people in the city who wrinkle up their noses and look indignant when they see us. *Care* is a creamy-white word so you would think that being *in* care would be a good thing, but it is the stuff of nightmares. That is what Skye says.

It seems the only useful thing I could tell Skye when she found me was my name, and even then it was incomplete. People who are not feckless, as we are, have at least two names: a given name and a family name. Their friends call them by their given name but the government and the police call them by both names, like the politician Joseph Lloyd, who wanted to build houses for the homeless and who has escaped to Scotland now. Skye says I probably had two names too, most people do to begin with, but all I could tell her when she found me was that I was called *Giorgio*.

When I was quite a lot smaller I did not like my name. When I started to play with the other boys they would call out to me, making the name sound long and silly: "Gi-or-gi-o!" they would shout, and I would stamp my foot and say, "*Not* Gi-or-gi-o!"

So one day I asked Skye if I could change my name, like Walking Tall had done. Skye laughed. "What would you like to be called?" she asked.

I thought about it, and about the person I wanted to be, and I thought about Walking Tall's name, so I said, "Running Fast!"

She laughed and tickled me a little behind my knees, the way I liked her to. Then she said, "But your name is special, Giorgi. Every name is special. Names are given for a reason, and we don't know why your parents called you *Giorgio*, but it must have mattered to them." I suppose she read the doubt on my face. "Maybe it was the name of your dad, or your grandpa, or someone really important to your mum and dad. Your name is a thing they gave you, and you shouldn't throw it away."

We were sitting on the old earthworks while we had this conversation, halfway round to the piss-pit, looking down the

Hill to the river and the wide, green meadows before you get to the city. I think I said, "But Walking Tall threw his old name away!"

"Ah," said Skye. "Yes. Well, it's rather different. He didn't throw his name away, he left it behind."

I thought about that while a couple of birds swooped low overhead and some tiny, blue butterflies settled on flowers close to my hand. "So, could Walking Tall go back and collect his name again, sometime, if he wanted to?"

Skye wrinkled up her nose. "He could," she said. "But I don't think he will. I hope he won't."

★ ★ ★

I do not remember anything about the time Skye found me, and I am not sure that the memories I have of before those days are proper memories, or dreams, or things I just made up. I think I remember someone rocking me and singing to me. I remember snatches of songs. Or did I hear them somewhere else, at this camp, maybe? One song said, *Bed is too small for my tired head,* and another asked, *How can I keep from singing?* We know lots of songs, on the Hill. We sing them round the fire in the evenings and mums and dads sing to help their little ones go to sleep. We boys have some songs with very rude words in them, about the police, and there is a man, called Music Maker, who has a guitar and sings lonely songs on his own, sitting up among the trees on top of the Hill. I think that Music Maker has lost someone he loves, as I have done, because so many of his songs are about someone who is no longer with him. One song is about all the things he can remember about the one he has lost, and then there is a haunting chorus, *but you're not there,* and another is about red lights in the night, as a girl drives away. Not all of Music Maker's songs are sad, though, or at least not in the lost sort

8

of way. *Sad* is a golden-yellow word and it has two different meanings. Sometimes, like when Music Maker sings about the girlfriend who is not there, *sad* means that you feel like crying. But when Music Maker sings the song that says, *I see the stars, I hear the mighty thunder, your works throughout the universe displayed,* then *sad* means something serious and still, something which is not so lost that you can never find it again. I once asked Music Maker if he would teach us the *mighty thunder* song, to sing round the fire, but he just smiled his odd smile (Music Maker does not have many teeth) and said, "No religion here, young Giorgio!"

I think that perhaps religion is allowed in the trees, but I do not really know what religion is, only that it causes lots of trouble. I cannot quite see how the *mighty thunder* song could cause trouble, but I am still quite young and learning something every day, so perhaps that is one of the things I will learn soon.

I wonder who Music Maker is singing to, in the trees? He is not singing to his lost girlfriend, because she is not there. I think he is singing to the Old Man, and I think the Old Man does not mind religion.

I wonder if those two bits of songs, *Bed is too small for my tired head* and *How can I keep from singing?* are things, like my name, that my parents gave me? I wish I could remember more.

★ ★ ★

The girls make daisy chains in the summer and wear them like crowns round their heads, or like beads round their necks. They make them for each other, and it is a sign of friendship. Once a group of girls, all giggling and pink, gave me a daisy chain because they said I was sweet, and I wore it round my neck. Little Bear said I was a sissy, but Big Bear told him to leave me alone. "You're only jealous," he said to Little Bear.

"Me, jealous of a daisy chain!" said Little Bear.

"No, jealous because the girls like Giorgio," said Big Bear.

"Oh, girls!" said Little Bear. "Yuk!"

It is a strange thing about boys and girls. While they are kids they do not much like each other, but when they are growing up they like each other a lot, and make shelters together, and sometimes have babies with a lot of screaming.

The grown-ups wear beads made out of wood or dried berries, and sometimes they have plaited threads round their wrists and sometimes they have shiny necklaces in colours which are too bright to be real, which they get from the market in Winchester. I asked Skye once how they get them, and she said, "Oh, they beg, borrow or steal." I can see how you can beg or steal from the market. I once stole a bottle of drink, when I was in the city with Dylan, and his mum did not know, but when I tasted it, it made my mouth hot and it was bitter, so I emptied the liquid down a drain, and Dylan has put the bottle upside down outside his tent, to show that the tent is his turf and nobody can go in without saying the password.

I do not see how a person could borrow from the market, though. I have tried to think how it would work. I can sort of picture how it would be. Let us say, I really liked a pair of socks I saw on a market stall. There are always socks for sale and they have bright colours and pictures of strange creatures which Skye says are cartoon characters, and I would very much like a pair of socks like that. So, I go up to the stallholder and he says, "Can I help you?"

Then I pick up the socks I like best, and I say, "I would like to borrow these, please."

Then how would it go? I do not think the man would say, "Certainly, young man. How long would you like to keep them?" I think he would tell me to scram, and maybe he would use some of the rude words we sing in our song about the police.

A few people have metal necklaces and rings. I think metal is cool. The word *metal* is grey but in real life metal can be silver or gold or bronze, and it is usually shiny, but on damp winter days it goes dull and then it is tarnished. The Music Maker has a metal chain which he wears round his neck, and on it there is a cross with a man stuck to it. Usually the Music Maker wears it inside his shirt because it is to do with religion, and religion causes a lot of trouble, but I have seen it quite often, if it is summer and he takes his shirt off, or if we go swimming in the early morning in the river, before the posh boys start practising in their boats. I am very interested in that chain and the cross and the man stuck to it, because I have something like that, too. Well, not quite like that, and anyhow, mostly Skye keeps it for me because she says it is important that I do not lose it, and boys will be boys. Skye says I was wearing it when she found me. It is a grey metal chain which shines if Skye breathes on it and rubs it with a piece of rag, and the thing that hangs from it is like a cross inside a letter Q. (Q is a beautiful colour: a shiny blue or green, like we see on kingfishers in the springtime.) The cross inside the Q does not have a man stuck to it. It is just plain, and it is the part that shines best when we polish it with our breath, because it is flat and easy to rub. Skye does not know what the sign means, of a cross and a Q fixed together. I worried for a while that it was to do with religion, and that my mum and dad were involved in religion and were causing a lot of trouble. I would not want to come from a mum and dad who caused trouble. But Skye says she has never come across this sign before and we should not jump to conclusions. She keeps the necklace with the cross and the Q in a little leather bag, in with her stuff, but if she goes away she gives it to the Old Man or to Walking Tall, in case she does not make it back.

★ ★ ★

So that makes three things which my mum and dad gave me before I lost them: my name, some words from songs, and a necklace which I will wear when I am older but not yet, because boys will be boys. Three is a special number, everyone says so, but Skye says they gave me lots of other things too.

"Everything we are, when we start out," said Skye, "comes from our parents." She said this when I told her that my mum and dad had given me three things. "Your dark hair and your brown eyes come from them, and your good brain, and your long legs (which she tickled, like she often did), and the shape of your fingernails. It all comes from your parents."

When I thought about that, I could see it must be true. One of the girls has a mum with dark brown skin, and the girl, who is called *Firefly*, has brown skin too, although not as dark as her mum. Big Bear and Little Bear both have fattish sorts of faces although they are not fat boys, and their mum has a round face too, and lots of smiles.

"So, if I found my mum and dad," I asked Skye, "would I be able to recognise them, because they would look like me? And would they know I was their boy?"

But Skye said it was not as easy as that. "If you knew they were your parents," she said, "you would probably see the likeness, but not if you just saw them across the street."

This is quite a disappointment to me, because I have a sort of dream that I think about at night as I am going to sleep, when I see two grown-ups in Winchester, across the road by the Guildhall. They would be holding hands and looking for me, because I had lost them, and they would see me and call, "Giorgio!", and run across to the flats where there was once an old bus station and hug me. But it seems that this is unlikely, if what Skye tells me is right.

There is a strange thing about the words *mum* and *dad*. Well, really it is just the word *dad*. These are words which crop up often, every day, and they are always the same colours, the way words are. *Mum* is a reddish word with smooth edges, and *dad* is a pattern of black and blue. But when I think about *my dad* it is quite a different colour. The words *my dad* are surprising, bright green and shiny, and I do not know why that is.

★ ★ ★

When I was still very small there were a lot of people living on the Hill, and some others who lived on the nature reserve. Skye says the nature reserve is a gamble because it is so close to the city and people like to walk there. "It's too easy for the cops, too," she says. "They just park where the feeding station used to be and they're in. Whereas," and she looks around at our camp, "nobody wants to come up here anymore, and we would see the police from miles away."

It makes me feel safe to think that we would see the police when they were still a long way away, then we would run and hide and none of us kids would be put into care, and none of the adults would go to labour camps or to prison. Sometimes, though, we do go to the nature reserve, up to the far end, as far away from the buildings of the town as we can get. We just do that when we have intel that some official body is going to clean up the Hill. *Intel* means *intelligence*, and it is a whitish word. Our intel comes from Scott who knows a girl who works in the city offices. Once, when we went back to the Hill, we found that they had recut the maze and put a sign up at the bottom of the Hill telling people the maze was up there. Some of the grown-ups turned the sign around so that it pointed explorers who wanted to see the maze in quite a different direction, and we were all careful to come up the Hill the back way so that there was no track for people to follow, and we did not have any trouble.

Now that I am a bit bigger, there seem to be fewer people living up here. I ask Skye about it, and she says I am old enough to understand now, and she takes me and Little Bear, who I am playing with, and we sit on the bank of the earthworks and she tells us what is happening.

"Do you remember what *government* is?" she asks, to begin with.

I know that it is a brown word, but I cannot quite think what it means. Little Bear is probably younger than me (except we do not know how old I am), but he knows. "I think government is the people who make laws and boss us around," he suggests.

Skye laughs. "Pretty much!" she agrees. "Well, the government of this country does not like people like us."

I know that is true. "We are the Scum of the Earth," I say, proudly.

Skye laughs even more and hugs us both. "Indeed we are!" she says, sounding very happy about it.

"Why don't they like us?" I ask. I think we are pretty cool people.

"It's hard to explain," she says. "Partly it's because we are poor. Partly it's because we don't see the world like they see it. Sometimes it's because we've criticised the government and the government hates to be criticised."

I think about that. "But if they don't like us because we're poor," I wonder, "why don't they give us money, and we would be rich!"

"Ah, now, there you have it!" says Skye. "Governments get their money from the people they rule. They make them pay a bit every month. It's called *taxes*. If the rulers want to help the poor they have to put up the taxes, so that people who are not poor have to give the government a bit more every month. And the people who are not poor don't like that."

Little Bear says, "I would not want to pay taxes, if I had any money."

Skye laughs again. "Exactly!" she says.

I do not think Skye's answer gets to the real problem. "But governments boss people around!" I point out. "People don't want to go into care or into labour camps, but they still have to go. Why don't they just *make* people pay more taxes?"

"Because, Giorgi my boy," says Skye, and puts her arm round me, "there are a lot of people who are not poor, and if the government makes them pay more taxes all those people could gang up together and get rid of the government, and choose a new one which did not make them pay more."

We all sit there on the bank and watch the cars humming along on a road a good long way away. The cathedral bells start ringing, and a ladybird sits for a while on Skye's skirt then flies away.

"So where have all the other people gone," I ask, "who used to live here?"

"Ah, yes, that's where we started," says Skye. "Well, boys, they haven't all gone to the same places. Some of the grown-ups are in labour camps and some of the children are in care."

I shiver at the dreadful thought of care. Little Bear says, "And where are the others?"

"Well, that's the thing," says Skye. "The others have mostly gone to the north, and a few to the west."

"Why?" I know about north and west, but I do not see what Skye is getting at.

"To the north," explains Skye, "a long way to the north, there is another country. It's called Scotland. And in the west, across the sea, is a country called Ireland. If people can get to those countries they can start a new life, and get jobs, and live in houses, and the children can go to school, and everyone can see a doctor if they're ill. So then they feel happier."

Little Bear says, disgusted, "But they'd have to pay taxes!"

Skye laughs again and ruffles Little Bear's hair. "Out of the mouths of babes…" she says, which makes no sense at all. Then she adds, "They can say what they really think in those countries. They know they will never be put in a labour camp, and their children will never be taken away from them for being feckless, and be put into care. They feel safe. That's why they go."

We all sit on the bank some more and give the matter some thought. After a while I say, "If I found my mum and dad I'd like to live with them in a country where we could say what we wanted, and go to school, and not be put into care." I think a bit more, and look up the Hill, where I can just see the thatched roof of one of the shelters, and the blue-grey smoke from a fire. "But I don't think I'd want to live in a house," I add. "I like our shelters."

"You wouldn't want to live in a shelter in Scotland," laughs Skye. "It gets pretty cold!"

So now, if people leave the Hill and don't come back, I think of them living in houses in Scotland and Ireland, and I wonder how they like living in buildings, and whether they miss those of us who have stayed behind.

★ ★ ★

I am sitting in our shelter now, thinking about all this. Skye is helping Martha and Dragon's Child make our evening meal, which will be pot-luck stew, made out of loads of different things they gleaned last night. Dragon's Child has her baby strapped to her back and so she has to stay out of the smoke. She is cutting up vegetables. Skye is stirring the pot. The Professor is sitting a little way away, drinking tea and reading a book. She has to peer at it very hard to see the words because her eyes are not what they were.

I am thinking about finding my mum and dad, and going to live, with them, in Scotland or Ireland. Since the conversation about the things they gave me, and how I might not just recognise them across the street, I have started to wonder whether I need to do something in particular to find them. I have just been learning about clues in our classes. A clue is a sort of sign, not a sign made deliberately, more an accidental sort of thing. For example, when the first crocuses come, that is a clue that winter is nearly over, and if a nearly grown-up boy and girl hold hands and kiss a lot, that is a clue that soon another baby might come into the camp. I have been thinking that although my parents gave me lots of things (like the shape of my fingernails, which is not at all a useful gift), they gave me three definite, proper clues about who they were. I do not know where to start, with the bits of songs, or with the necklace and the Q with a cross and no man stuck to it, but I could start with my name. So, I think I will go on a quest, like King Arthur and the Knights of the Round Table who used to live in the Great Hall in Winchester, and who left their table behind when they went away, and I will find my parents by following up the clues.

CHAPTER 2

My Name

I do find the Old Man a bit scary. He wears camouflage trousers and a grey cap, and he has a long grey beard, and long grey hair which he puts in a ponytail tied up with a black shoelace. Except on the hottest days of summer, the Old Man wears a sort of blanket with a hole in the middle for his head, and there are things sewn onto the blanket – small pieces of coloured cloth and little bits of embroidery, making signs, and a coin with a hole in it which comes from another country a long way away. He does not say much. If we kids ask him questions he usually tells us to go and ask one of the grown-ups, so there is not a lot of point in us going to see him, but every now and then one of the adults will look at something we have done in our classes, or something we have made, and they will say, "Go and show the Old Man."

Then we have to go up the Hill beyond the last shelter, which is where Big Bear and Little Bear live, into the trees beyond where the girls play, and we have to call, "Old Man! Old Man!"

Usually we hear a sort of grumpy noise and it comes from the ring of logs in the middle of the trees, where the Old Man has his fire and where grown-ups sometimes go to discuss important things that are not for little ears. Sometimes, though, the Old Man is by the maze. He grows some plants there, to use for medicine or tea, and to make good smells.

Then we have to say, "Skye told me to show you this," or

"The Music Man told me to say my nine times table to you," or whatever it is.

Then the Old Man looks very seriously at the thing we have made, or he listens very gravely while we recite our tables, and then he says something quite short and nice, like "Well done, Giorgio," or "I couldn't do that when I was your age."

It is a great privilege to be sent to see the Old Man. Round the fire at night mums say to dads things like, "Firefly was sent up to show the Old Man her poem today," and then Albi, or whoever the dad or the partner is in that case, says, "Wow, Firefly. Well done! May I see it too?" and everyone round the fire smiles and is pleased.

Once Big Bear was sent to see the Old Man for something quite different. He had not learnt a good thing or created something original; he had pushed Limpy over the earthwork and Limpy had fallen a long way and bumped his head. Walking Tall gave Big Bear a huge telling-off and said he must not pick on people smaller than him, especially not someone with a handicap, but Big Bear was angry and said that Limpy kept pushing in on our game (which was true) and that he used bad words (which I think was not true – anyhow, I had not heard them). When Walking Tall found that Big Bear was really not sorry, he told Florence, who is Limpy's mother, that he couldn't get through to Big Bear and that he was going to go and see the Old Man.

We all watched as Walking Tall climbed the Hill and went into the trees. Big Bear said, "He can't do nothing. Let's get on with our game."

But Little Bear, Dylan, Mikki and a couple of others who were there at the time were not so sure, and we did not feel like going on with the game at all, so we all sat in a row on the earthwork that Big Bear had pushed Limpy over, and waited to see what would happen.

After a while Walking Tall came back down the Hill and headed straight for us. "Right, Big Bear," he said, his voice all serious, "the Old Man wants to see you, NOW!"

We all jumped because Walking Tall does not often sound angry, and Big Bear got up without any further arguing and walked up the Hill with Walking Tall until they reached the trees, then he went on, on his own.

He was gone a long time, and we had a lesson about the bones in our bodies, before Big Bear came back. We learnt how Limpy had been hurt by the stick a policeman carried, when he was still a babe in arms and his dad had taken him on a demonstration, and how he had been allowed no medical care because his dad was unemployed and was a militant socialist, and if they had gone to the hospital Limpy would have been put in care. Limpy showed us what he can do and what he cannot do with his bad leg, and he let us feel the big, bony lump just below his knee, and we all thought he was a bit of a hero.

Then Big Bear came back down the Hill, and he had definitely been crying. He came straight up to us, and said without any prompting, "I'm sorry, Limpy. I shouldn't have pushed you."

And Limpy said, "That's okay."

Then the guy who was taking our lesson, whose name I have now forgotten, said, "Do you mind this crowd calling you *Limpy*? You must have another name, don't you?"

And Limpy groaned, and said, "Yeah, *Blessing*! I'd rather be called Limpy!"

In bed in the shelter I asked Big Bear what had happened on the Hill with the Old Man, and Big Bear said, "I'm not talking about it."

So I asked, "Did he hurt you?"

Then Big Bear sort of snorted under his blanket and said, "No, don't be silly. He's a good guy, the Old Man. A really good guy." And that is all he would say.

★ ★ ★

Because of the incident with Big Bear and Limpy, it is a really hard decision to go and see the Old Man. To be honest, it is taking all my courage, even though Big Bear says the Old Man is a good guy, and he should know.

I would rather question someone else, really. I tried Walking Tall, who I am staying with while Skye is away, and he just said, "I'm sorry, Giorgio, that's not really my field of expertise." Then I asked Music Maker and he said, "I don't think you're old enough to start all that sort of thing, yet. Give it a year or two." I even asked Dragon's Child, who was sitting in the sun playing with her baby, who had no clothes on, and who was sucking her toes, but Dragon's Child said, "I didn't go to a proper school either, so I don't know how you would do a thing like that."

So now I'm climbing the Hill to find the Old Man, who I think will know what to do.

I am in the shade of the trees now. It is special up here, a sort of quiet place. You can hear the wind in the leaves and you can hear a plane flying overhead, making pollution, and there are birds singing. In the summer the leaves ripple in the breeze, but they all fall off in the autumn, and the wind howls in the branches, but the Old Man is always here.

"Old Man, Old Man!" I am shouting, standing quite close to the maze so that he can hear me whether he is sitting on a log by his fire, or tending his plants.

At first there is no reply, and I am just beginning to wonder whether, for once, the Old Man is not here, when suddenly here he is, right in front of me, just a few feet away.

"Hello, Giorgio," he says. He knows all our names.

"Hello, Old Man," I reply, looking down at my feet and wondering whether this is a good idea.

"You want to ask me a question," says the Old Man. I have not told him that, he just knows.

"Yes."

"Come and sit down," he says, and we go to the log circle where the fire is, and he stirs up the wood with a stick and hangs a billy can over the flames to heat up some water.

I do not say anything. He makes a sort of sign with his hand, that I am to sit down, and then he just gets on with making his herb tea.

When he is done he passes me a tin mug smelling of mint, and drinks some of his own, and still he does not say anything, and nor do I. I am not frightened, but I am shy.

Then he says, "You are thinking about your parents."

"Yes," I agree, and we sit there some more.

"It is hard for a boy not to know where he comes from," says the Old Man.

"Yes," I agree.

Again, we are quiet, then he asks, quite kindly, "What is your question, boy?"

I hope he will not think I am silly. I say, "My parents gave me my name. Giorgio. I want to know why."

The Old Man looks as if he is thinking about that. I think I had better make my point more clearly. The Old Man is very quiet, but it does not feel cheeky for me to go on.

"Skye says that names are important. Perhaps I am named after my dad, or my grandpa, or someone who was important to my parents."

"Ah, yes," says the Old Man. "Skye is right."

Again we are silent. A rabbit hops into the clearing with his nose twitching and then hops out again.

"So," says the Old Man at last, "you think if you can find out why your folks called you *Giorgio*, you would be one step closer to finding out who they were?"

"Yes," I agree, and wait.

"It is a big task," says the Old Man. "And you are still a small boy."

I think about that. "Small boys like to have mums and dads," I say.

The Old Man chuckles.

"Let's start with the possibility that they named you after someone important," he says. "Perhaps you need to find out about all the famous people called *Giorgio*. And *George* too, because that's the English word for *Giorgio*. How does that sound?"

I think about it, and finish my tea. The Old Man is not in a hurry. He stirs his fire and puts some more wood on it. Then he says, "Skye will be back the day after tomorrow. She will be able to help you."

I go back down the Hill and Big Bear says, "Where have you been?"

I say, "I went to see the Old Man."

Big Bear says, "You didn't!" but I can see on his face that he knows I did.

★ ★ ★

Sure enough, two days later Skye is back in the camp.

When Skye goes off on her journeys she takes a backpack and a walking stick, and when she comes back she sometimes brings people with her, although not so much nowadays, and she sometimes brings interesting things and even gifts for people. This time she has brought a teenage girl who has dark black hair and a tattoo on her very white arm, and a book which she tells us is an atlas.

They build a shelter for the girl with the black hair near to the shelter where Dragon's Child and Sputnik live with their baby, who does not have a proper name and is just called *Baby Girl*. I think that it is a good name for now, but that Baby Girl will not approve of her name when she is as big as me, only when I say as much to Dragon's Child she says, "She can choose her own name then." That seems fair enough to me, except that Skye told me that your name is a gift your parents give you, and I think Baby Girl has a right to that gift too.

I am not very interested in the teenage girl, and I think it is weird that she has a tattoo. Usually it is only old people who do that to their skin. Skye says that it was a fashion a long time ago. I am interested in the atlas, though. It is a big book, really heavy to carry around, and it has maps on every page, of all the countries in the world. Skye says it is a little out of date. It shows that Greece is still in the European Union but they have left now, like we did, although they have not joined up with the USA, which is good, because joining the USA is a retrogressive step. *Retrogressive* means going backwards, and it is a maroon word, but if I look at it for a long while in my head it loses its colour. Skye says I might grow out of seeing these colours, and if I do, I think the process might start with *retrogressive*.

The grown-ups say we will have lessons about other countries now, since we have the atlas, and us kids are quite excited. Firefly wants to know all about Jamaica because her grandmother came from there, and Big Bear, Little Bear and I want to know about Scotland and Ireland, in case we go to live there sometime, and are free to say what we think, and have to pay taxes. Nobody wants to learn about the USA because people always say that they have trodden on our country with a Big Boot, but Skye says, "All the more reason why you should learn about them," and Walking Tall reminds us that people are just people and we should not judge others by what their governments do. "After all," he says, "our government puts people in labour camps and in care, and we wouldn't want to be judged by that, would we?"

What with all the excitement about the atlas and the girl with the tattoo, and with building a new shelter, and with having chocolate spread for dinner, brought back by Skye, we do not have time to talk about my ideas until we go to bed.

★ ★ ★

Our shelter started off as a tent a long time ago. It was orange and green, with a zip to close the door, and strings called guy ropes to stop it from blowing away if it was windy on the Hill. The good thing about the tent was that we could take it down and put it up again somewhere else, like on the nature reserve, but there were bad things too. When I was little there was plenty of room for Skye and me, and it was comfortable knowing she was right next to me. But as I started to grow bigger we found it harder to fit ourselves in, with Skye's backpack and my toys. Also, the zip broke, and then rain started to come in at the far end, where our feet went at night. So then lots of people in the camp did a rebuild. A *rebuild* is when we enlarge or mend someone's shelter. They took the guy ropes away and they cut and then lifted the orange and green material, which is called canvas, so that it all became the roof. They put sticks and plastic down the sides and they put thatch on the roof, and rows of sticks along the sides, so that from the outside it looks like a wooden shelter, but inside you can still see the orange and green canvas.

Inside, Skye made a sort of partition with some red patterned cloth which does not go with the orange and green, like the words *Wednesday* and *Thursday* do not go together. *Wednesday* is brightly coloured in spring greens and yellow, a bit sparkly, and *Thursday* is a very dull maroon colour, almost brown, which is ugly. I sleep on one side of the red cloth and Skye sleeps on the other, so we have our own rooms but I can still hear her snoring at night, and she knows if I have a nightmare and can just reach out and touch me. Another good thing about our rebuilt shelter is that we can both sit up in it, so when the weather is bad we can stay inside without having to lie down.

We are in our shelter now and it is quite late. Skye has been telling the others about things that are going on in other parts of the country and people have been talking about whether the government will fall. Skye says not, because it is propped up by the Americans, but Walking Tall says the Americans cannot last forever.

I am in my sleeping bag with my clothes folded under my head to make a pillow, and Skye is doing something to her hair. I am just settling down to sleep when Skye says, "Did you go and see the Old Man, Giorgi?"

I turn over onto my back so that I can see the ceiling of the shelter, which looks black in the dark, not orange and green.

"Yes," I tell her. "This morning."

Skye says, "That was very brave of you! Do you want to tell me about it?" Then she says, "You don't have to tell me anything if you don't want to."

Of course, I do want to. I tell her about my conversation with the Old Man, and about my need to find out about important or famous people called Giorgio and George.

Skye thinks for a bit, and I hear her wriggling into her sleeping bag. She puts her walking boots outside the shelter because they smell, and says, "I hope it doesn't rain tonight." Then, when she is settled, she says, "I am proud of you, Giorgi!" I hear her turning over. "You can start tomorrow," she says. "It will be a proper bit of research."

She starts to snore before I go to sleep, and I like the sound. I say the word *research* to myself and it is a mixture of reds, like the tiles on a roof. Then I go to sleep too.

★ ★ ★

The grown-ups – Skye, Walking Tall, the Professor and Spanner-in-the-Works – talk over breakfast about my research. Walking Tall thinks all of us kids, once we can read and write, should do some research, and the Professor thinks that this is a good idea, but she wrinkles up her nose. "Honestly," she says, "it's good for kids to follow up their interests, but how can they? They need reference materials, a device or two and access to the internet…"

Little Bear and I are eating the last of the chocolate spread on stale crackers which were left outside Little Bear's shelter. His mum says to Skye, "Do you think they should be eating that stuff for breakfast? It's not very good for them."

But Skye says, "Once it's gone, it's gone." Then she looks in the jar and says to us, "Leave the rest for Big Bear." Big Bear is still sleeping because he went gleaning with Walking Tall last night.

The Music Maker walks past. He has his guitar on a strap round his neck, and I think he is going up into the trees to sing to the Old Man.

"Morning all!" he says, and touches his forehead as if he is wearing his hat. "This all looks very convivial."

Little Bear picks up his wooden knife, which he made last summer, and is about to take some more chocolate spread, but Skye puts her hand over the jar and says, "Big Bear's!" Then she says to the Music Maker, "We are talking about the kids' next project."

Music Maker squats down in the gap between the Professor and Walking Tall. He says to me, "Chocolate spread? For breakfast? The Lord have mercy on your body!" Then he says to the grown-ups, "I thought they were going to study countries? I was all up for teaching them about California in the '60s."

Skye laughs. "Flower power?" she says, which does not make any sense to me.

27

The Professor says, "Giorgio here wants to find out about his name. We thought they could all do some research of their own, but there's the problem of resources…"

"Ethnographic work," says the Music Maker.

We all look at him. He might as well have spoken a different language.

He explains. "Sociologists do it," he says. "Instead of using books, they study groups of people, first-hand. Our kids can start their research by interviewing people here, in the camp."

Everyone is quiet for a moment, thinking about that. The Music Maker says, "Anyhow, I need to be off," and he stands up and heads up the Hill.

The Professor says, "That's a good place to start, you know," then she adds, "although it's not ethnography." I wonder whether it is always comfortable to know as much as the Professor knows.

Skye says to me, "Would you be happy to start there, Giorgi? You could ask each person about any famous Georges or Giorgios they might have heard of. Someone right here might have a clue about your parents, without even knowing it!"

I have finished my last chocolate-coated cracker and am feeling a bit too full. I take a swig of water from one of the glass bottles that the People Who Must Be Saints leave for us near the bottom of the Hill. "I need to be able to write it down," I say. "Or I might forget."

The Professor looks angry, but not with me. "Honestly," she says, "what sort of country would deny its children simple reading and writing materials? It makes me want to—"

Walking Tall puts a hand on the Professor's arm. "Not now, and not here," he says quietly, looking at us kids. Big Bear has come out of their shelter and joined us by the fire. He is holding the nearly-empty jar of spread and sticking his finger in to scoop out the chocolate, then eating it straight off his finger without spreading it on the crackers.

The Professor goes, "Hmph!" and uses her stick to help herself stand up. She walks down the Hill a bit and round, to the place where her shelter is built. Her floaty black scarf has come half undone from around her neck, and it blows behind her in the breeze.

"It's going to rain," says Spanner-in-the-Works, who is good at telling the weather.

Skye says to me, "We'll see about getting you all some notebooks."

"And pens?" I ask.

"And pens," agrees Skye.

★ ★ ★

Dylan, Little Bear and I went into a shop in Winchester once, not long ago. It is a shop in the High Street which is also a post office, for buying stamps and sending parcels. The shop assistants do not like us to go into their shop. They say we are Little Buggers who will steal anything we can lay our hands on. It was a Saturday and lots of people were going in and out of the shop, so they did not see us. It was late August, and in September all the kids whose parents are not feckless go back to school. The shop was full of stuff for the rich parents, who are not feckless, to buy for their rich kids, who may go to school whenever they want. Everything was brightly coloured: pens, notebooks, little boxes and bags for putting pens and pencils in, rubbers and pencil sharpeners and plastic things for stapling paper together, loads of things. There were shelves of devices for going onto the internet to find things out and to send emails, in many different colours and sizes, with *50% off* on one whole stack full. I do not know if we are Little Buggers, because I do not know what that

means, but we do *not* steal everything we can get our hands on. Skye says that in an ideal world we would not steal at all, but "needs must," she says, which means that if you are feckless, and you have no benefits and no rights, you do not get much choice.

So I am sort of hoping that Skye will turn up, today or tomorrow, with coloured notebooks and pens like the ones we saw, to help us to do our research. In the meantime, Music Maker is going to teach us about California in the 1960s, which is a lesson with lots of music in it, and some singing. We have to have our lesson in the shelter that the bikers left behind, when the Old Man said that they could not smoke pot here and they would have to go. It is a large shelter but it only has walls on two sides because they did not finish building it. We use it mostly when it is raining, as it is now.

★ ★ ★

At dinner this evening we are all talking about our research. Some of us know exactly what we want to do. I want to find out about the name *Giorgio*, of course, and *George*, which is the English form, and Firefly wants to research Jamaica, which will include using the atlas, but also talking to other people. At first Little Bear wants to research the name *Justin*, because his mum told him that his real dad was called Justin, and Little Bear knows I am researching a name which might have been my dad's real name. But Little Bear's mum says, "You don't want to do that, Little Bear. He was nothing but a waster. A bully and a waster. Research something else."

That has put Little Bear into a muddle because he does not know what else to research. Then Walking Tall says, "Why don't you do research about food?" and Little Bear looks happy, because food is a really good subject. Big Bear wants to research songs and music, after the Music Maker's lesson about California yesterday, and I am almost envious of him, because perhaps that could have been my second choice. If I researched music I might find out about *Bed is too small for my tired head* and *How can I keep from singing?* Then Skye says that in a month we will all do presentations, which is when each one of us will tell the others what they have discovered, so if Big Bear does find out a clue to help me, I should learn about it then.

We are all quite excited, but a bit disappointed when they tell us we still have to do maths and English as well. Never mind, I especially like numbers, which are a sort of magic.

★ ★ ★

I suppose I knew really that they would not be able to get us those coloured notebooks. It is the following morning and we have had an English lesson about adverbs, which describe verbs, like *he walked hurriedly* or *she spoke grumpily*. Both these things are true today because it is still raining and we have to rush from one shelter to another to stop ourselves getting too wet, and the people doing the cooking are grumpy because the smoke from our fires does not go straight up in the air on days like this. It sort of hangs around, and gets in your eyes, and makes you cough.

And here comes Spanner-in-the-Works, walking up the Hill with his hood up and a bin liner full of stuff over one shoulder. He waves cheerfully to us and shouts, "Join me in the big shelter!"

We all go over to the bikers' shelter and Spanner-in-the-Works puts his bin bag on the ground.

Everyone gathers round. Spanner-in-the-Works puts his hoody, dry side up, on the ground and starts to take things out of the bin bag and put them in neat piles on the hoody. There are lots of things, but none of them are brightly coloured, and my heart sinks. Sometimes I really wish my parents had not been feckless, and I could have colourful notebooks and a box with a sliding lid to keep my pens in. Even so, there is quite a selection of useful items.

On one pile Spanner-in-the-Works puts writing pads. These have large sheets of paper in them which tear out easily. There is a smaller pile of notepads with curly wire round the top. He has two big folders you can open and put paper into, or take it out, and three green plastic envelopes with studs on them, for keeping things safely inside and not dropping paper in the mud by mistake. He has two orange boxes which are full of pens. Skye says, "Spanner?" in a sort of doubtful tone, as if she is not quite happy about those pens, but Spanner-in-the-Works winks at me and says, "They were past their sell-by date."

Then he reaches into his bin bag again, and he has a small pile of proper school notebooks. They are not brightly coloured, they are maroon and bottle-green, like a fir tree in the autumn. Spanner-in-the-Works says, "These aren't new, but they've got lots of clean pages in them."

We all lean over the pile of notebooks. They each have a crest on the front, and the words, *St Mark's Primary School*. Then, underneath, *The home of excellence*. I open the top one. Someone has been writing on the first and the second page, and the rest is blank. It is nearly new. I don't like the dark green, but I like the cleanness of the rest of the notebook, and I think it will do nicely for my research.

Then Dylan says, sounding really excited, "Hey, Giorgio, this one has your name on it!"

He passes me a maroon notebook. It is not my name on the cover, but it is the English version of my first name, and somebody else's family name. *George Pearson*, it says, and then the letters 'VIP' which have been crossed out in red. Inside, George has been making lists of words. I think they might be for spelling tests. The words are easy and I wonder if George Pearson is younger than me. I give the green notebook to Dylan in exchange for George Pearson's maroon notebook.

Skye says, "Where…?" and does not finish her sentence.

"Most of the stuff comes from that office supply shop," Spanner-in-the-Works says, sitting back on his heels in a sort of squatting position. "The one near the top of town. It was piled up outside the back door, in boxes. I had to go through quite a lot of stuff because the top things were all soggy from this blessed rain."

"They weren't throwing out the pens," suggests Skye, who is looking a bit unhappy.

Walking Tall says, "They're really cheap, Skye, those sorts of pens. I wouldn't worry."

"The notebooks," Spanner-in-the-Works goes on, "are another matter altogether. I came back past St Mark's and thought I would just check their bins, and what a find! Kids," he says, looking at us, "you have these notebooks at the taxpayers' expense! As is your due!"

I do not know what he means, but I do not mind.

Skye says to me, "Do you want to tear out the first few pages, Giorgi? Then you will have a perfectly clean book to start your research."

But I say, "No, thanks." I like to think that a boy with a name nearly like mine has started the book, and I will go on with it. "I like this notebook just as it is."

"Altogether," says Walking Tall, "a pretty good bit of gleaning. Thanks, mate."

"You're welcome," says Spanner-in-the-Works. "I'll just pop up and talk to the Old Man."

★ ★ ★

The Professor says we should do our work in an orderly way. Walking Tall says, "They're just kids, Professor!"

But she insists. She talks to each one of us about how we are going to conduct our research, and she wants each kid to have one adult they report back to as they go along. "It's how these things are done," says the Professor, and although Walking Tall has a grumpy look on his face he does not argue. Dylan is going to report to the Professor about his weather research, and Little Bear is going to report to Dragon's Child. Dragon's Child is not very happy about this at first. She says, "I haven't had no education!" but Skye says, "No, but Little Bear is researching food, and you're the best cook in the camp!" Baby Girl gurgles as if she agrees, but I do not know how she would know. She just drinks milk.

I expect that Skye will be my research adult but she says, "I might need to go away again, quite soon." I suppose I look disappointed, so she says, "Who would you like to report to? If it could be absolutely anyone in the camp?"

I think about this. I like the Music Maker a lot but he is the one Big Bear will report to, and anyhow, does he know much about names? I like Walking Tall too, but I do not think of him or Spanner-in-the-Works, as people who know lots of things. I know who I would really like.

"Can the Old Man be my adult?" I ask.

Everyone looks surprised. They say things like,

"Well…"

"But…"

"The thing is…"

And "If it were not for…"

And none of them finishes their sentence.

Then Skye says, "We could always ask him."

All the others look at each other, the way grown-ups do when they are giving a matter serious consideration.

Then Walking Tall says, "Why not?"

And Skye says, "I'll go and see him now," and heads off up the Hill.

34

Big Bear says to me, "You're crazy!" But I think I am not.

I wait in the shelter Skye and I share until she comes back out of the trees, looking happy. I go to meet her. She is smiling. "He says yes," she tells me, and gives me a hug.

★ ★ ★

Before I can go to see the Old Man again I have to have a plan. The Professor makes us all write our plans on the first clean page of our notebooks. We have to have a goal and a methodology. A methodology is a way of doing things. It is a maroon word, almost exactly the same colour as my notebook, and I think that this is a good sign. I write:

Goal: To find out as much as I can about famous people with the name Giorgio or George.

Methodology: I will talk to everyone in the camp (except Baby Girl) and ask them to tell me about anyone with those names that they know about.

I show this to the Professor and she says, "It's good as far as it goes. Why aren't you going to ask Baby Girl?"

I think she is nuts. "Baby Girl is just a baby!" I point out. "She cannot talk and she doesn't know anything!"

"Right," says the Professor. "You know that, and I know that, but a stranger reading your research would not know that. Always write your research as if a stranger were going to read it!"

I think this is a bit silly, but the Professor is quite particular about the way things are done, and she is giving us all a lot of help on this project, more help than I think she has ever done before. So I say, "Okay," and I add after *Baby Girl* the words *because she is not old enough to talk yet.*

★ ★ ★

When I go up the Hill to show the Old Man I think he is waiting for me. The billy can is already bubbling over the fire and there is a different sort of tea, not mint, this time. He looks very seriously at my goal and my methodology, and he smiles, I think because of the bit about Baby Girl not being old enough to tell me anything yet.

Then he says, "Have you thought about where to start?"

I say, "With the grown-ups, whoever is not too busy."

"Sensible," he says, and goes on drinking his tea. Then he adds, "There might be one or two people you don't feel like asking. Perhaps you don't feel close to them, or you think they won't know anything. Don't fall into that trap, Giorgio; you'll be surprised at what some people know."

We both drink our tea for a bit more, then he says, "I hope you'll be surprised, anyhow."

So I say, "Thank you, Old Man," and pick up my notebook and go back down the Hill.

★ ★ ★

The Music Maker is coming up the Hill, in the opposite direction. He is carrying his guitar and humming to himself. When he sees me he says, "Finished with the Old Man for now?"

"For now," I agree. Then I see my opportunity. "Please can I ask you some questions, Music Maker?"

He looks a bit doubtful. He says, "I need to fix my spirit first." Then perhaps he sees me looking disappointed, and he says, "Give me half an hour. I'll see you by my fire."

I cannot tell when half an hour has passed because I have not noticed the cathedral clock strike, but I say, "Okay," and I go down to Skye's shelter.

"Are you really going away soon?" I ask her. She is looking carefully at her walking boots, to see if there are any holes or weak bits.

"I'm afraid so," says Skye. "Sorry, mate." Then she says, "You're all right with Walking Tall, aren't you?"

And I think about it, and I say, "Yes, I'm good with Walking Tall and I'm even better with the Old Man."

Then Skye laughs and looks relieved, and gives me a hug.

"Where are you going?" I ask her, although I know she will not tell me.

"There and back, to see how far it is!" she says, and we both grin.

★ ★ ★

I sit by the fire, which has been damped right down for the day. It is not raining, but the sky is grey and I need my jacket, which is a bit small for me but quite snugly. It used to belong to Big Bear. I can hear the Music Man in the woods at the top of the hill, fixing his spirit. He is singing songs which are not too sad. He sings the *mighty thunder* song more than once, then he is very quiet, and then he sings another song. I can only partly hear the words. *Oh come, oh come, Emmanuelle...* I think that Emmanuelle must be the woman he has lost, and I think that she will never hear him, singing for her to come back, if he sings quietly like that in the woods. I think he ought to go down into the city and busk on the pavements, and sing there, and perhaps Emmanuelle will hear him, or her friend might hear him, and go to Emmanuelle and say, "Music Maker is singing for you to come back."

When he comes down the Hill, Music Maker looks quite happy, like his normal self. He comes straight over to Skye's fire, and he says, "Right, Giorgi, fire away!"

At first I do not know what to ask him. I say, "I am researching my name. Giorgio, or George."

"Right," says Music Maker.

Then I think, *The Professor told us to ask specific questions.* A

37

specific question is a question that the person cannot answer in a woolly way. I say, "Can you tell me about the most famous George you know about?"

"Ah," says the Music Man. "Indeed I can."

Then he tells me about a man called George Harrison. George Harrison was part of a singing group. They wrote and sang lots of songs, together, then they split up and all went their separate ways. "George Harrison was the quiet one," says Music Maker. "Quiet and spiritual."

"Spiritual?" I ask, because that is a golden and silver word but I do not know what it means. If I look at the word sideways it has flecks of shiny red in it too.

"His spirit came alive," says the Music Maker, "when he went to India."

I am a bit lost. "Was his spirit dead before he went to India?" I am a bit concerned. I am not sure what a person's spirit is, exactly, but I do not like to think that anyone could go around with something dead inside them.

Music Maker smiles at me. "No, not dead," he reassures me, "just asleep. Nobody's spirit is dead, whatever they might say."

I think about this. "How did he know his spirit had woken up?" I ask.

The Music Maker thinks and drums his hand on the wooden part of his guitar. "I hope I'm not teaching you religion..." he says.

Inside our shelter Skye says, "You're all right, Music Maker," and I realise she has been listening all along.

"I think he felt it," says Music Maker, smiling towards the shelter and answering my question. "And then he wrote a song to say how he was waking up." Then the Music Maker plays on his guitar and sings, only very quietly, about his sweet lord, and about wanting to serve him, and I wonder who this lord was, and why anyone who is free, and who lives in a shelter, would want to serve another person, even a lord.

Skye crawls out of the shelter and stands up. She is smiling at Music Maker and I think her eyes look a little watery.

I feel a sort of gentleness inside me. "Was that George a good man?" I ask.

"He tried to be good," says Music Maker. "And that's all we can hope for, in this life."

I think about that. "Do you think my parents might have called me *Giorgio* after that George?" I asked.

"If they did," says the Music Maker, not exactly answering my question, "then you are the carrier of a noble name and you should try to live up to it. And it would mean that your parents had taste and discernment."

I do not know about taste and discernment but I can tell that they are good things, and I feel proud. I think probably my parents *did* call me after that George, and I think that my research is going really well.

Then Skye says, "Can you sing 'The Tax Man' to Giorgi? I think it will amuse him."

So Music Maker strums his guitar and starts to sing, and I see Little Bear up the Hill by their fire, and I call, "Little Bear, Little Bear, come and listen!"

Then Little Bear runs down the Hill to our fire and listens to Music Maker, and Music Maker sings a really funny song about a tax man taking lots of money from people. It is funny because the tax man is cheating people, but it is also funny to think of a man, a real, living man, collecting taxes, when I expect that it is all done by a droid in real life. If a proper man did it, as in the song, I think that he would have no friends.

"Yeah!" says Little Bear and we insist that Music Maker teaches us all the words until we can sing it from beginning to end, and everyone is laughing, and other people gather round the fire and some join in. Then Big Bear comes and says, "*I'm supposed to be doing research about music!*"

And the Professor says, "This does not sound like serious study to me!"

Then the group breaks up, and Music Maker takes Big Bear off for a lesson, because he is going to teach him how to play the guitar, and Little Bear wanders over to Dragon's Child's fire to learn about cooking, and I start a new page in my *George Pearson* notebook, and put the title *George Harrison* and write down all the things Music Maker has told me.

★ ★ ★

The next day I think I will talk to Sputnik. Sputnik often goes out in the daytime, gleaning or looking for work *off the books*. This means that the people who pay him for doing the work will not write it down in a book, or on their devices, or anywhere at all, so that the police and the anti-terrorists will not be able to track Sputnik down. Today, though, he is at home by his fire, holding Baby Girl and talking seriously to Dragon's Child.

Dragon's Child looks upset. She is saying to Sputnik, "But I don't know *how* to look after babies!"

And Sputnik says, "But shouldn't it come naturally? Doesn't everyone know how to look after a baby?"

Then Dragon's Child says, "Well, I don't! I'm useless! You look after her," and she goes away, round the Hill, and Sputnik is holding Baby Girl, and Baby Girl is crying.

I hesitate. I think this might not be a good moment to do research with Sputnik. But he sees me standing there, and he says, "Hi, Giorgio!" in a perfectly normal voice, so I say, "Hi!" back and sit down on one of the log seats by their fire.

Sputnik says, "Don't worry about Dragon's Child. She's had a tough time, you know. She never had a mum and dad."

"What, *never*?" I say, wondering how Dragon's Child could have come into the world without a mum and dad.

Sputnik says, "She grew up in care. She didn't get any love. Now she doesn't know how to love Baby Girl."

"Anyhow," he says, patting Baby Girl on her back and then rocking her up and down in his arms, "what can I do for you?"

"I'm wondering," I say, getting straight down to it, "whether you remember any famous Georges? Or Giorgios? For my research."

"Well now, let me think," says Sputnik. "My best friend at school was called George, but he wasn't famous."

"Did you go to school?" I am amazed. "Aren't you feckless?"

Sputnik laughs, then says to Baby Girl, who is asleep and cannot hear him, "Did you hear that, Baby Girl? This boy, here, thinks I may not be feckless!"

Then he says to me, "Giorgi, boy, I'm as feckless as they come!"

I think this needs to be followed up. I always thought that being feckless was a thing you were born into, like being English, or being foreign. I say, "So when did you become feckless? After you finished school?"

Sputnik looks away, rocking Baby Girl gently and frowning a bit.

Then he says, "I was sixteen. I had two years left of school. My brother Joe was eighteen, just taking his Senior Baccalaureate. My dad worked for the council and we had a house and a car. Mum worked in the library."

He goes quiet. I think he has forgotten I am there. After a bit I prompt him, "Then what?" I ask.

Sputnik looks back at me and sighs. "Then they outsourced all the council jobs," he says. When he sees that I do not understand, he says, "They asked a private company to do the work, for much less money. They offered my dad his job, exactly the same job, for the minimum wage, and Dad wouldn't do it. He said it was a matter of principle."

Baby Girl is sucking her thumb very noisily, still asleep. Sputnik looks down at her and says, "Look at that!" and kisses her forehead. Then he goes on:

"So Dad tried to find other work, but it was all really badly paid. We were trying to live off Mum's money and pay the mortgage, and there just wasn't enough. Mum went to the feeding station by the river until they closed it down, and Joe took a night-time job as a guard out by the American base, and fell behind with his studies. Then we were evicted from our house." Sputnik looks at me, and explains, "Thrown out."

He is frowning as he remembers. His voice goes quiet and gruff. "They said my dad could have found work but he was too picky, so we weren't eligible for any benefits. They put him in a labour camp so that he would learn social responsibility. Joe joined the army, so he is not feckless. Last I heard, he was out in the Caribbean. Mum and I went to live in a shelter – not a shelter like ours, here, but a shelter for homeless people. Then the shelter people said that Mum was not looking after me in a responsible way, so I would have to go into care. So I ran away. And I have been feckless ever since."

I think Sputnik's story is very sad. "So where are your mum and dad now?" I ask.

"Heaven only knows," says Sputnik. "That was years ago."

I go back to the George who was Sputnik's best friend at school. "Didn't your friend try to help you? Your friend George?"

Sputnik suddenly looks more cheerful. "Oh yeah!" he says. "He did. He helped me to run away. He hid me in his garage for three weeks without his parents finding out, and brought me food, and gave me some of his clothes. But then the counsellor at school started asking him lots of questions about where I might have gone to and whether he had heard from me, so I moved on."

"So would you say your friend George was a good bloke?" I ask.

"Oh yes!" says Sputnik. "The best."

Baby Girl is beginning to wriggle and cry. "She wants feeding," says Sputnik. "I'd better go and find Dragon's Child." He gets up and walks off round the Hill in the direction Dragon's Child went earlier.

I go back to our fire. There is nobody there. I start a new page, and write *Sputnik's friend George.* Then I write down all the things Sputnik told me. I think that Sputnik's friend can have nothing to do with me being called *Giorgio,* but on the other hand it is good to know that this George, like George Harrison, was also a good guy. I am beginning to think that my name is a good name to have.

Then Walking Tall calls us all together to have an English lesson, and I tuck my notebook under my sleeping bag and go to their fire, where we will do creative writing until snack time.

★ ★ ★

I am in my sleeping bag, but Skye, Walking Tall and Little Bear's mother are sitting round our fire, and I can hear them talking. They have gleaned a bottle of wine and they are passing it round from one to another, drinking straight out of the bottle and laughing quite a lot. They start talking about us kids. Little Bear's mum says, "They've been singing that blessed song all day!"

"Which song?" asks Walking Tall, who left the Hill right after our English lesson and only came back, with the bottle of wine and some other stuff, just before dinner.

"'The Tax Man'," explains Skye. "Music Man taught it to

Giorgio and Little Bear this morning. Now all the kids are singing it."

Everyone laughs. It is strange, the way adults are amused if we do things, but they would not be amused if grown-ups did the same things. Still, it is nice.

Then I hear a sort of odd, muddled noise and several people taking at once. I hear Skye say, "Sputnik!" and Walking Tall's woman say, "My God, what's happened?" Then Walking Tall says, "Is it Baby Girl? Is she ill?"

I hear Sputnik. It is his voice, but it sounds strange. "She's gone! She's gone!" he says, and I hear that he is crying.

"Sit down, mate," says Walking Tall, trying to sound calm but sounding a bit panicked all the same.

"Who has gone?" asks his woman, Little Bear's mum, almost at the same time.

"What do you mean, *gone*?" asks Skye.

"I can't bear it," says Sputnik, and he is really crying, like Limpy cried when he was pushed over the earthwork.

Skye says, sounding really calm like the Old Man if he has to consider a falling-out between two people in the camp, "Sputnik, can you tell us what has happened?"

Sputnik is sobbing. I can hear him. I wriggle up in my sleeping bag, closer to the door of the shelter, so that I can see what is happening. They are all black and yellow shapes in the firelight. I see Walking Bear put an arm round Sputnik. Skye and Little Bear's mum are standing up, as if they are getting ready to do something right now.

Sputnik says, still sobbing, "Dragon's Child. She's taken Baby Girl away."

"What?" they all say, not believing it. I feel a sort of bump in my chest as my heart suddenly beats harder.

"I should have seen it coming!" says Sputnik.

Skye says, "Where has she taken the baby, Sputnik? Do you know?"

I think Sputnik must have nodded. I cannot see a lot because the fire is dying down and it is a black night. Then he says, "They've gone to the mother and baby clinic at the hospital."

"What?"

"Why?"

"But…" Nobody can quite believe it.

"Was Baby Girl ill?" asks Little Bear's mum, sounding confused.

"N – no," sobs Sputnik. "She's taken Baby Girl there so that they will put her in care!"

Everyone goes very quiet. For the first time, I notice the crackling of the fire. Then Little Bear's mum says, "My God!"

Again, everyone is quiet. Sputnik says, at last, "I should have seen it coming."

"What happened?" asks Skye, quietly. I stick my head right out of the shelter so that I can hear everything. The grass is wet with dew.

Sputnik is also talking quietly, as if he is talking to himself. "She really wanted that baby," he says. "She thought it would make us a proper family. But when Baby Girl was born she didn't know what to do. She didn't know how to raise a child. I told her I would help her. I told her it was easy, we just had to love her, but Dragon's Child – she was not so sure."

"We were all here to help," says Little Bear's mum.

Sputnik says, "She thought she would hurt Baby Girl. She thought that one night, if Baby Girl cried, and if I was not there, she would hit Baby Girl, and make her slow, so that she couldn't learn anything."

"Why did she think that?" asks Walking Tall, sounding perplexed.

It is Skye who answers. "Because she grew up in care," she says, and she sounds bitter. "She never saw children being brought up with love. She saw children being hit and abused, or just left alone to fend for themselves. She never learnt to trust her own judgement."

Sputnik says, "That's right. The stuff she told me…"

I think Little Bear's mum starts to cry. "That poor baby," she says, and I do not know if she is talking about Dragon's Child or Baby Girl.

"That's why she wouldn't let me choose a name," says Sputnik. "I wanted to call her *Morning Star* but Dragon's Child said the chances were someone else would give her a different name by the time she was three. She never believed we could keep her."

Walking Tall asks, "When did she go?"

Sputnik answers, "While I was out gleaning with the lads. Earlier this evening."

Walking Tall says, "She will already be at the office, then. All the offices for the feckless are open in the evenings. There's no point in trying to do anything tonight."

Sputnik cries some more.

Walking Bear says, "Come on, mate, let's you and me go for a walk. Right?" Then he picks up the bottle they were passing around before this horrible interruption, and waves it in the air at the others, and puts an arm round Sputnik and leads him away into the night.

Soon Skye climbs into her sleeping bag.

"What will happen to Baby Girl?" I ask her.

"Goodness, are you awake?" she says. "Did you hear all that?"

"I did," I say.

Skye says, "It's a tragedy, but perhaps we shouldn't be surprised."

"I am surprised," I say.

"Yes, I suppose you are," says Skye. Then she says, "If children grow up without being loved it damages them for the whole of their lives. They don't know how to love, or how to behave. So then they do things that hurt other people – and that hurt themselves, too."

I think about this.

"Will the care people hurt Baby Girl?" I want to know.

"I hope not," says Skye. "Not intentionally."

"Accidentally?" I ask.

"Yes, probably," says Skye, sounding very sad.

I think for a bit.

"What will they do to Dragon's Child, Skye?" I want to know.

Skye sighs and turns over so that I know she is facing me, on her side of the partition. She reaches through and strokes my hair. "I think they will put her in a labour camp," she says.

★ ★ ★

It is hard to get on with our research next day. Little Bear has to have a new grown-up to help him, now that Dragon's Child has gone. Nobody quite knows who to ask, but then Sputnik says, sort of quietly, "I can cook. My mum taught me. Shall I help Little Bear?" and everyone looks pleased, and Walking Tall says to Sputnik, "Atta guy!" which means something I don't understand, but which is good.

I learnt a lot from talking to Sputnik the day before, and I am glad I spoke to him when I did, because I suspect he might not have been so happy talking today. He is helping Little Bear but he does not look as if he is thinking about his words, or about cooking. I am sure he is thinking about Dragon's Child and Baby Girl, who should really be called *Morning Star.* I wander round the camp thinking about who to ask next. Walking Tall and Skye go together to talk to the Old Man about Dragon's Child and Baby Girl, and later Walking Tall goes back up the Hill with Sputnik, while we kids are learning maths with Dylan's dad, who used to teach it in a proper school until they thought he was subversive. It is Dylan's dad who first showed me that numbers are magic, and I like it when he teaches us, although Big Bear says it is too hard.

After the maths lesson, when we generally have snacks (which the Professor calls *lunch*), I decide I will question Dylan's dad for my research. We are all sitting round Dylan's fireplace although their fire has gone right out. Big Bear is practising chords on the Music Maker's guitar, and the dark-haired girl who arrived with Skye last time she came home is sitting with Sputnik because Sputnik is sad.

I ask Dylan's dad the usual question about whether any famous Georges or Giorgios spring to mind, and Dylan's dad says, "Mm, unfortunately, yes!" He tells me about two American presidents, father and son, and about the things they got up to. He makes them sound like very evil men. Then Spanner-in-the-Works says, "Mind you, they were fairly elected."

Walking Tall says, "They were certainly elected, but whether it was fair or not..." and Dylan's dad tells me all the ways Americans have managed to stop black people from voting, all through the ages, even though they are equal to everyone else and America is supposed to stand for equality.

"Can we vote?" I ask, because I know what voting is but I have never thought about being able to vote for a president, or a prince, or a prime minister, or whoever rules us.

And Dylan's dad says, "No, not us!"

"In the old days we would have been able to," says Walking Tall.

"Would we, though?" asks Spanner-in-the-Works. "I mean, could people of no fixed abode vote? I know prisoners couldn't."

"Good point," says Dylan's dad in a way that said, *I don't really want to discuss this.* Then everyone – all the grown-ups – tell me bits and pieces about the George Bushes, for me to write down in my research book, and then we start talking about wars and there seems to be nothing else to say about George Bush Senior or George Bush Junior, so I go and write it up. Then Little Bear and I invent a new game with Limpy called *Gleaning,* where we try to take things from other people's fire circles, and we play until the shadows are long and Sputnik calls Little Bear to come and help him cook dinner.

★ ★ ★

I would have known that Skye was getting ready to go away, even if she had not told me. She goes up to see the Old Man more often, she has sorted out her walking boots, and Little Bear's mum has asked me to pass her my dirty shorts and pants, so that she can wash them with Big Bear's, Little Bear's and Walking Tall's. She takes them all the way down to the bottom of the Hill, to the river, and washes them there, early in the morning before the dog walkers come or the posh boys practise their rowing. When Little Bear's mum does my clothes washing it means I am a part of their family.

I am continuing with my research. People have told me about lots of different Georges, and I am beginning to think it must be quite a common name in the world where people have two names, a given name and a family name. I am told there is a King George but he lives in Washington DC, which is in America, for half the year, and in Buckingham Palace in London for the rest of the time. He is our king but the Americans like him to live in their country as a sign that we are all one now. Someone tells me about a famous and excellent football player called *George Best* who lived a long time ago, and for a day or two Little Bear and I play football on the grass below the maze. The Hill, however, is not a good place for playing football because the ball keeps rolling down towards the river and is only stopped by the earthworks. Also, we do not know the rules, and our ball keeps losing its air and going flat.

The girl with the dark hair, who arrived here with Skye, has a given name and a family name. Like Sputnik, she was not born Scum of the Earth, but has only just become feckless. She tells me she was at the art school by the park, and that she got fed up and just walked out. At first she uses a lot of very bad words, worse words than the ones we sing in our song about the police. Then Skye takes her up to see the Old Man, and she is there for a long time, and when she comes back down she is sorry about the rude words, and does not say them as much anymore, and if a rude word slips out she says, "Woops!" and covers her mouth with her hand. Her given name and her family name are Cheryl Matthews, but Skye tells me she will get a new name soon, when she is ready.

"Could she go back to the art school, and not be feckless, if she wanted to?" I ask Skye.

"Perhaps," says Skye, who has a map spread out on the grass and is looking at it carefully.

"Why did she start to be feckless?" I want to know.

Skye looks up from her map. "To be honest, Giorgi, I don't think she is feckless, not in the real sense of the word. She's damaged. But then, that's the way it goes." She looks at me and smiles, and says, "You're too young to understand all this, Giorgi. Don't worry about it. Cheryl will be okay with us, for a while."

I see Cheryl talking to Sputnik. The day after Dragon's Child left, when she sat with Sputnik, I thought she wanted to be his woman, and I thought, *Not a chance! Sputnik loves Dragon's Child*. Then I noticed that when the Professor lost her glasses and could not see to read her books, it was Cheryl who looked all over the Hill, and then found them just where the Professor had left them, by her fire. I think she is someone who preserves things, which means she stops them from going bad. Someone taught us, once, that there are creators, preservers and destroyers. Each is important, and each has a little of the other two in them. So when I go and see the Old Man about my research, I say to him that I think that Cheryl is like the person in the myths, the preserver, and that perhaps her new name should be Vishnu. The Old Man smiles and says, "Vishnu is a man's name." Then he says, "Leave it to me," and after he has talked to her, she is called Vishna, which sounds female, and she is my friend although she is grown up.

Vishna knows about lots of Georges, and the ones she knows seem very interesting. She says that there was a George who had his last name as George and his first name as Lloyd. He was a good bloke who tried to make it so that everyone in the country, rich or poor, could see a doctor or get medical treatment whenever they needed. Vishna tells me that this system lasted for years and years, and only ended after we left Europe and Scotland left us, and we joined up with America and they did not like socialised medicine. So now, after all those years, the feckless people like us can no longer see doctors unless, Vishna says, we have the cash in our hands. She says that Lloyd George must be turning in his grave, and I laugh, because I can imagine being in a cemetery in the night-time, and all the earth on top of Lloyd George starts moving, like blankets when you turn over in the night.

It seems that Lloyd George was a very good man. Altogether, the Georges in my research book seem more good than bad, and I am pleased about that, although I am no closer to finding out about my mum and dad than when I started.

★ ★ ★

I climb into my sleeping bag, thinking *Tomorrow night I will be sleeping next to Little Bear.* Skye has been round all the campfires talking to people. She will try to find out about their friends and relatives who are not feckless, to see if they are doing all right, and she will make contact with Useful People. When she has finished doing the rounds, she climbs into her sleeping bag.

"Goodnight," I say.

"Aha!" says Skye, "You're still awake!" Then she says, "Giorgi, what would you do if I didn't come back?"

I think about that. The thought of Skye not coming back makes me feel sad and lonely, but I say, "I suppose I would live at Little Bear's."

"And you would be good, and do what Walking Tall told you, and be polite to Little Bear's mum, wouldn't you?"

"Yes," I say.

"And you would tell the Old Man if you had problems, and not bottle them up?"

"Yes," I say again, feeling very uncomfortable inside.

"And you would be very, very careful if you went down into the city, and not cross the police or be cheeky to people in the street?"

"Yes," I agree again. "If you didn't come back I'd be really careful. But I want you to come back."

"Me too," says Skye, and we both go to sleep.

★ ★ ★

Then it seems about ten minutes later, although you cannot tell because time is different when you're asleep. Suddenly Skye and I both wake up at exactly the same moment, because there is a huge crash right over our heads, and a flash of lightning, and another crash followed by a long, continuous rumble.

"Uh-ha!" I say to Skye. "A thunderstorm!"

"I should say!" says Skye, and pulls the red curtain back

so that I can see she is sitting up in bed. "Pretty close, I would say."

I am not frightened of thunder. It is just nature's way of clearing the air, one of the bikers once told me. Skye is not frightened either, but she is concerned. "We haven't dug a trench round Vishna's shelter," she says. "I hope it doesn't rain too hard."

Usually when we build a new shelter we dig a trench round the top and the two sides, so that if water comes rushing down the Hill it will not pour into the hut, but instead will follow the ditches either side of the shelter and go off down the Hill without making someone drenched through and through. When we put up Vishna's shelter, the ground was very hard because although it had rained when Spanner-in-the-Works went gleaning for our research books, it has actually been a very dry summer.

No sooner has Skye said this than it starts to rain. It rains really, really hard. We can hear it on the thatch of our roof, and quite quickly we can hear the water gurgling in our trench, and Skye says, "I'd better go and check out the damage."

"Can I come?" I ask, but just then there is another big crash of thunder, and Skye does not hear me. I get out of my sleeping bag anyhow.

The best thing to do, if it is raining really hard, is to go around the camp barefoot. Feet are easier to dry than shoes and less likely to slip on wet grass. If we do not have anything to keep out the rain we wear black bin liners, but I have a waterproof jacket which I wear on top of my sleeping shorts. I follow Skye out of the shelter.

Everyone seems to be awake. There are children crying but also talking in excited voices. There are grown-ups checking their own ditches and putting bin liners over places where their thatch is not keeping the rain out, and Skye is climbing the Hill towards Vishna's shelter. Walking Tall is already there with his big spade, digging a ditch for all he is worth. Big Bear is helping him.

Nobody seems to be bothered that I am out of my shelter. Big Bear shouts to me over the thunder, as if I am a grown-up, "Oh, hi, Giorgio. Can you clear that muddy patch so that the water flows more easily?"

So I take a sort of trowel that he gives me, and I follow behind Walking Tall. Walking Tall digs a deep ditch with his big spade, but the bottom of the ditch is rough. I take out all the mud that gets churned up by the water that is trying to catch up, all the while, with Walking Tall's spade, and I heap the mud beside the ditch on the side away from the shelter. Quite quickly the job is done and the water is pouring down the Hill.

We all stand up and Walking Tall says, "Wow!"

Big Bear and I high-five each other, because Vishna's few possessions have been saved from a soaking.

Skye looks across the valley towards the city, and shouts, "This is quite a storm!"

We all stand there in the pouring rain. The sky is cracking and rumbling enough to make you deaf, but it is the lightning we are looking at. It seems just to go on and on, flickering over the city and over the Hill, sometimes like a big flash, sometimes like a sparky line of light, dancing over the city.

Big Bear screams, "Dad, I think the cathedral's been hit!"

But Walking Tall shouts, "Oh, it'll be okay. They fit lightning conductors."

The rain keeps pouring down. In our camp children are looking out of their shelters. Nobody can go to sleep through this, we think. Then Big Bear's mum yells, "Has anyone seen the Professor?" and no one has, so she goes to check.

She comes back a few minutes later, squelching over the soaking grass in her bare feet, and says with a laugh in her voice, between crashes of thunder, "Sleeping like a lamb!"

Then we all settle down, here and there, in our shelters or in the big tent left by the bikers, and we watch the storm. I think of Music Maker's *mighty thunder* song, and I understand that thunder really is mighty, and it makes me feel joyful, sitting with Skye, watching the lightning.

★ ★ ★

The storm seems to be going away several times, and then comes back. "It's circling around," says Skye, and that makes it sound like an animal, a living creature who wants to attack us. After a bit, though, despite the amazing lightning and the crashing and banging, I start to feel sleepy again, and I lean against Skye and I go fast asleep.

And when I wake up, it is over.

It is quite late in the morning. I can tell from where the gleam of the sun is. It is not a clear, bright sun; it is watery, behind vapour in the sky.

The camp is busy. People are rethatching roofs and clearing out ditches. Some are rebuilding fireplaces. All the fires must have gone out in the night, but Dylan's dad has relit theirs, and other people are walking across to their shelter with bits of dry wood, to carry fire back to their hearths. They stop at Dylan's shelter for a while and drink tea, and a few people smoke fag ends and everyone chats in quiet voices. There are no classes today because there is too much rebuilding to do, and Skye says she will not go for a couple more days, until everything is shipshape.

Skye has only just relit our fire and there is no hot food yet. I sit in my sleeping clothes on a damp log and eat crisps from a packet that the People Who Must Be Saints gave us a night or two earlier, and drink water from a bottle. Then I check my *George Pearson* notebook. It is still dry, just a bit crumpled because I keep it under my sleeping bag at night.

The Professor comes over, leaning on her walking stick, with her black scarf knotted round her neck like a big, floppy tie. She is wearing her glasses round her neck too, on a piece of thread which Vishna plaited for her, so that she does not lose them again.

Skye stands up when the Professor approaches.

"Morning," she says.

The Professor eases herself carefully down onto the highest log, using her stick to balance. Skye goes to help her, but the Professor says, "No! No! I'm all right. I'm not an old lady yet!"

I think she is not quite telling the truth, because she is actually quite old, but I do not say so.

The Professor says, as she settles herself, "Well, would you believe it? I slept through the whole storm!"

"I know," says Skye, laughing. "We went to check on you."

"Thank you kindly," says the Professor. Then she says to me, "How's the research going, young Giorgio?"

I am surprised that anyone is thinking about research after such a momentous storm, but I say, "Good, thank you."

The Professor puts her glasses on. She asks, very politely, "May I see?"

I go back into the shelter and pull my book out from under the sleeping bag. I pass it to the Professor, turned to the first page where it says my goals and my methodology.

She reads my notes carefully, peering a bit because I have small handwriting and the Professor's eyes are not what they used to be. When she has read it all, she says, "The part about Lloyd George is interesting. Who told you that?"

"Vishna," I say.

The Professor looks pleased. "Vishna is a very interesting young lady," she says. "Or she will be, when she grows out of all that adolescent angst." Then she says, "Ask her to tell you about Giorgio Armani. He should be part of your research."

56

Skye says, "Tea, Professor?" but the Professor is struggling to her feet.

"Not now, not now!" she says. "Places to go. People to see."

Then to me she says, "It's time you were up and dressed, Giorgio. Cultivate a little discipline!"

Skye winks at me behind the Professor's back. I think she is right, and go into the shelter to find my red shorts and my black T-shirt with the hole on the shoulder. They are my favourite day clothes.

★ ★ ★

By snack time things are getting back to normal. Spanner-in-the-Works has gone around to each shelter and has asked, politely, whether they need any help putting things to rights. Ditches and trenches have been redug and bits of black binliner are having new thatch put over the top of them. The fires are lit and there is hot food for those who want it. Vishna has built her own hearth now, so that she no longer needs to share with Sputnik. Sputnik is mostly eating at Walking Tall's fire now, anyhow. He and Little Bear are doing quite a lot of the cooking, which Little Bear's mum says is interesting, and Little Bear is writing all the recipes down in his research book ready to report back to us.

I ask Little Bear how he's enjoying his project. He says, "Well, it's good." Then he says, "Did you know that grown-ups cry?"

I did know that. I had heard Sputnik crying the night Dragon's Child had taken Baby Girl away, and I had seen tears in Skye's eyes when Music Maker had sung 'My sweet Lord'.

"They're only human," I say, and feel very grown up myself.

Little Bear says, "Sputnik talks about Dragon's Child and

Baby Girl a lot. He says, 'Dragon's Child taught me how to cook this and I had hoped I'd be making this for Baby Girl, one of these days.' And he cries. And I don't know what to do."

I think about that. I used to cry when Skye went away, and Little Bear's mum used to cuddle me, but I was just a little one then. I think about grown-ups crying, and what we should do. I have no real experience.

I say, "Didn't your mum cry when Justin, your real dad, went away? What did you do then?"

Little Bear says, "Mum didn't cry. She said, 'Good riddance to bad rubbish!' and she took us to a burger place in town and spent the very last of our money, and then we came up the Hill to live here."

I find that interesting, but not helpful in thinking what to do when grown-ups cry. I think of the night Dragon's Child left, and the way the other grown-ups behaved round Skye's fire, and I say, "Perhaps you should just pat Sputnik on the back?"

Little Bear looks at me as if I'm crazy. "He's six foot tall!" he says.

★ ★ ★

Now that we have had our snacks, the grown-ups are making plans. Skye says, "Perhaps we should go down into the city to see how things are there?"

Little Bear's mum says, "Why? They don't care how things are for us!"

Then she catches the eye of Walking Tall who is giving her the same sort of look he would give one of us if he caught us dropping rubbish in the camp. "Well!" says Little Bear's mum, "it's true!"

Walking Tall says, "There were two families in the nature

reserve last week. It's very low-lying. We ought to check on them, too."

"I think they're weed smokers," says Vishna. "I know a couple of them."

"Well, then, they can't come here," says Skye, "but we can still help them. If necessary."

Spanner-in-the-Works says, "There might be some good gleaning, too. If people were flooded."

"Let's go and see," says Skye.

I say to Little Bear, "Shall we go too?"

Little Bear says, "They won't let us." Then he says, "Me and Dylan are going to dig a paddling pool, so that if it rains again we can paddle in it. You can help us, if you want."

I think this will not work. The Hill is chalk beneath a thin layer of earth, and the water will just drain away. I do not say so, though. Instead I say, "I'm going with the grown-ups," and I put my trainers on, because if people see you with bare feet in the city they will think you are feckless, and put you in care.

★ ★ ★

I think that really Skye would not want me to go into the city today, but most of the adults who are going have already left. Vishna is talking to the Professor, who cannot manage the walk anymore, so I say as she leaves the Professor's fire circle, "Can I come with you?"

Vishna looks a bit doubtful. She says, "Do you think Skye would mind?"

I say, "Yes, but I really want to go and look at the city after the storm."

Vishna laughs. She says, "Did you get up and help dig the trench round my shelter in the middle of the night?"

"Yeah."

"Well, then, I think I owe you," says Vishna. "But if I say *run* you run, and if I say *hide* you hide. At once. Without any questions. Okay?"

"Okay," I agree, and we set off, a good ten minutes behind the others.

★ ★ ★

It is always exciting to go down into city. It is a bit dangerous, and it is quite strange, because it is hard to know what people are thinking and what they really mean when they ask questions. Most people are just busily going about their business. Some look as ragged as we do, or even more so, and Skye says those are the JAMS. *JAMS* are people who are just about managing. They are not feckless, and so they are better than us. Their kids go to school and they can see doctors if they are ill, but Skye says that they always feel, at any moment, as if they might fall through the cracks.

"They hate us more than anyone else," says Skye, "because when they see us, they see what they might become."

Skye tells me often, "When you walk around in the city, hold your head up. Walk tall. Look as if you have every right to be there. People are easily taken in."

Vishna and I walk alongside the river to get to the city. At first it is meadowland, with people going for walks with their dogs, and Vishna says, "Good afternoon," very politely, and they look a bit surprised but they smile, and say, "Good afternoon," back to us. This is because Vishna is acting as if we are respectable, and not Scum of the Earth.

We walk past the Bishop's Palace and through the gardens, still staying right by the river, until we get to the old, narrow bridge where they put traffic lights not long ago. Everywhere we go, we see signs of the storm. It seems worse down here in the city than it was up on the Hill, and that is strange, because surely we were closer to the thunder and lightning than they were?

There seems to be destruction everywhere. "Destruction and mayhem," says Vishna, and *mayhem* is a new word for me, a lovely blackberry red, and I say it to myself as we walk along. *Mayhem, mayhem everywhere!* The river, by the bridge with the new traffic lights, is lapping onto the footpath, and you can tell from the wet grass that it must have come much further up than that. There are bits and pieces washed up on the path, and people taking photographs and looking amazed. We turn left to the statue of King Alfred, and everything looks normal until we look into the Abbey Gardens and see big pools of water on the grass. The shops underneath the flats where the old bus station used to be all have their doors open, and people are sweeping mud and dirt out into the street.

Vishna says, to a lady with orange hair, who is looking despairingly at the shelves in her shop where all the device casings she sells are wet and bedraggled, "You seem to have been hit hard."

The woman gives a sort of grunt, and says, "The second time in as many years. When I bought this place, they said floods would be a one-in-a-hundred-years event. Huh!"

"Are you insured?" asks Vishna, sounding very grown up.

"Thank God, yes!" says the orange-haired woman. "But it's all the fuss of starting all over again. I thought this would be a nice little business to see me into my old age…"

Vishna says, "Can we help?"

The woman looks at us properly for the first time. "No, love," she says, "but thank you. Were you badly hit?"

"Hardly at all," says Vishna. "We live on higher ground."

I want to giggle. I do not think this woman would be so nice to us if she knew *which* higher ground we lived on. But we do not stand out today. Lots of people look bedraggled, and we are both wearing shoes.

It is the same story all up and down the High Street. It seems that two different catastrophes happened. One thing was that there was so much water in the river that it went over its banks and flooded houses and a pizza restaurant. The other thing was that such torrents of water poured down the High Street that it invaded shops and soaked everything that was close to the ground. There are piles of wet things beside the benches where people sit to make phone calls and to say to the person they have gone shopping with, "Where are you? I'm in the High Street opposite F&F," or "Okay, I'll see you at the car park in ten minutes."

A man is shouting at a police officer. "Where were the emergency services when we needed you?" he yells. "I'm ruined! Nobody came to help!"

The police officer is staying calm. "We were evacuating houses by the river," she says. "Human life comes before property, you know, sir."

The man is not impressed. His face is red and his forehead is sweating. "But I'm ruined!" he exclaims again. "Look in there!" and he points to his café. "Ruined!"

"I'm very sorry, sir," says the officer. She does not look angry although the man is shouting at her, because he is not feckless. If one of us shouted at her we would be arrested for causing a disturbance.

She says, "The mayor has requested assistance with the clearing up, if that is any help?" she says.

The man stops shouting. "What sort of assistance?" he says in a voice that is doubtful but eager at the same time.

"A labour crew," says the officer. "From the South Stockbridge Labour Camp."

The man still looks interested, but he says, "They'll steal everything they can get their filthy hands on!"

The officer says, "They'll be very well supervised."

The man says, "Well, I'm prepared to give them a try," as if he is doing the people in the work crew a great favour, instead of the other way around. "What will it cost me?"

"Oh, nothing," says the officer. "You've already paid for their services through your taxes. Shall I put you on the list?" And she gets her little droid out and starts talking into it.

When she is done she says, "Right. That's sorted. Will eight in the morning be too early?"

The man is still not happy. "I don't want any murderers in the crew," he says, "or sex offenders."

"No, no!" reassures the police officer. "These people are just work-shy. Taken off the streets to be re-educated. You're doing society a favour if you give them some real work."

"Well, in that case…" says the man. "And if it won't cost me anything…"

"No, no! Not a cent!" says the officer, and off she goes to speak to a woman who is gazing in at the closed pharmacy and looking worried.

I say to Vishna, "Do you think Dragon's Child will be in the work crew?"

Vishna holds my hand, not like a girlfriend, and not like Skye. Like a big sister, I think. "That's what I was thinking," she says.

Vishna has some money in her skirt pocket. We go into a shop by the market where they sell milkshakes which you can drink in the café or take away. We sit at a table with a red and white checked tablecloth. I have never sat in this sort of place before and I feel quite grand. When the girl comes to take our order Vishna says, "Two chocolate milkshakes, please," as if we have every right to be there, and the waitress says, "Right you are. Terrible storm last night, wasn't it?"

Vishna says, "Awful," and we wait for our milkshakes and drink them slowly, looking out of the window at smart people and just-about-managing people, kids out of school because of the flooding, business people talking into their devices and women with babies in buggies. Then Vishna leaves her money on the table and we wander out, giving our waitress a wave as we go, and head back toward our Hill.

And after all that, we are still home before all the other grown-ups.

★ ★ ★

The talk at dinner is all about the work crew. The grown-ups know Vishna and I went into the city because Vishna tells Skye at once, as soon as they all arrive home.

Skye says, "Hi, kids, had a good afternoon?" and Vishna says, "I took Giorgio into the city."

"You did?" says Skye, and I cannot tell from her voice whether or not she minds.

I am glad Vishna is telling the truth. I say, "We had a milkshake. One each. Sitting down."

Skye sort of laughs, and says, "Was it good?"

"Uh-ha," I say.

Skye says to Vishna, "You bought it?"

Vishna says, "I still have some money. Was that okay?"

"Of course," says Skye. "Good. The kids need to know how the world works, in case they ever join it again."

Vishna says, "Oh!" Then she smiles at Skye and says, "I didn't think of that; I just wanted a milkshake!"

Then they both laugh, little chuckles, and I wonder what is so funny about wanting a milkshake.

Then Vishna says, "They're bringing in a work crew tomorrow, to help clear up."

"Yes," says Walking Tall, "I heard that too."

"From South Stockbridge," she adds, as if that means something.

Sputnik looks at Vishna very sharply and says, "South Stockbridge?"

64

Walking Tall says, "She might not be there, Sputnik. They could have put her anywhere."

"And even if she's there," says Walking Tall, "it doesn't mean she'll be part of the work crew."

"Even so…" says Sputnik, and I know he wants to go back into the city the next day to see if he can find Dragon's Child.

Then they talk about work crews, and chain gangs in America, which is where the idea comes from, and paying them nineteen cents an hour, which is not enough to buy even one fag, and about work crews undercutting free workers, so we become bored, and Little Bear takes me to see the paddling pool which he and Dylan have dug. I am sure it will not work.

★ ★ ★

I want to go into the city again the next day, to see the work crew for myself, and to see if we can find Dragon's Child and rescue her. Skye says to me, "You know, Giorgi, she may not want to be rescued," which is an odd thing to say, and she says to Sputnik, "The world is a very frightening place if you've always lived in an institution."

Even so, Sputnik goes off down the Hill. He borrows a smarter jacket from Spanner-in-the-Works and wears shiny shoes, and he borrows the Professor's briefcase, so that he looks like a just-about-managing man, not like a feckless individual. We all wish him luck, and then the Professor says, "Have these children stopped studying altogether?" and we know that we are back into our normal routine.

I have several pages full of notes about different Georges, but the Professor had said, "Ask Vishna about Giorgio Armani." I think this is the ideal moment. Vishna is squatting at the Professor's fire. They are looking at the books the Professor turfed out of her briefcase, in order to lend it to Sputnik.

Vishna is asking, "And can you read Greek?" and the Professor is saying, "A little. I really need a Greek-English dictionary but I lost it, somewhere along the line."

Then they see me, and the Professor says, "Ah-ha, here comes our great researcher!"

I say, "Good morning, Professor. Would it be convenient for Vishna to tell me about Giorgio Armani now?"

"Ah!" says the Professor. "Very nicely asked. The days of good manners have not fled entirely!" To Vishna she says, "Go ahead, young lady. There stands the future of our nation." And she takes her glasses off her nose so that they hang round her neck, and looks away across the valley, although I do not think she can see very much.

Giorgio Armani is the first person I have been told about who is actually called *Giorgio* and not *George*. I am full of excitement in case this Giorgio turns out to be something special to do with my mum and dad. Vishna says, "I'll tell you what I know," and she tells me about him being Italian, and being a fashion designer, and earning a lot of money, and about how the best stores in London and New York stocked his designs. I write it down, but I feel a bit disappointed.

"So was he a *good* man?" I ask.

"He was a very gifted man," says Vishna.

I think about that a bit, and I ask, "But do you think a mum and a dad would call their boy after him, because he was gifted?"

Vishna says, "Not unless they were really into handbags. And perfume!"

I say, "I don't think I want a mum and dad who are really into handbags and perfume."

Vishna says, "We don't get any choice. My mum and dad are really into right-wing politics and military support groups."

Then she must notice that I am looking worried, and she

says, "But I can't believe your parents called you Giorgio after a handbag designer! I wouldn't worry, if I were you!"

★ ★ ★

The Old Man is tending his herbs when I go to see him. He is talking to them, encouraging them to grow, and congratulating them on new leaves. I stand and watch him, and then I ask, "Do they understand you?"

The Old Man stands up. "They don't understand my words," he says. "But they understand my care."

"That's like babies," I say, as we walk through the trees to his fire.

He stops and looks at me, and I think he is surprised. He says slowly, "You are absolutely right."

He waves at me to sit down, and blows on his fire to make it flare up to boil water. "Mint, I think, today," he says.

Then he asks, "Talking of babies, how is Sputnik today?"

I am surprised the Old Man asks me this. I always feel he knows everything already.

"He cried the night Dragon's Child left," I say. "And Walking Tall took him round the Hill to let him get it out of his system, but he still cries."

The Old Man says nothing. I think of Sputnik, who walked around the city all day looking for Dragon's Child in the work crews, and did not find her.

"And how are you, now that Skye has gone?"

"I'm okay," I say, and it is true.

"Living with the Bears," he says, stating a fact and thinking about Big Bear and Little Bear.

"Yes," I agree. Then I add, "Little Bear is learning to cook."

"And Big Bear is learning to play the guitar," says the Old Man. "What a gifted bunch you all are!" Then he says, "And how's the research?"

So we talk about all the Georges and the one Giorgio in my *George Pearson* notebook, and we drink the mint tea, and the Old Man stares into the smouldering fire. There are questions I would like to ask him, not about my research but about him, the Old Man himself. Then I think it would be cheeky, and before she left, the evening before the storm, when Skye said, 'Goodnight,' to me, as I was snuggled up next to Little Bear, she said, "And remember, Giorgi, treat the Old Man with respect!"

So I ask no questions, and we sit quietly until I have finished my tea, and then I say, "Thank you, Old Man," and I go back down the Hill.

★ ★ ★

Things have changed a bit since Skye last went away. I am still friends with Little Bear and Big Bear, but especially with Little Bear. Big Bear is having a growth spurt and suddenly seems much bigger than us, nearly as tall as Walking Tall, and he spends a lot of time playing Music Man's guitar. He goes gleaning with the adults at night, too, and I saw him smoking a fag end with Spanner-in-the-Works. Little Bear is doing a lot of cooking with Sputnik, but he is also playing with Dylan. They have made up a rain dance so that it will pour and fill their paddling pool with water.

I sometimes play with Little Bear and Dylan and they are always friendly, but I like to go across to Vishna's fireplace, and if Vishna is at the Professor's I wander down there. Vishna and the Professor talk about artists and writers and about the things Vishna was studying at the art school before she dropped out and became feckless. The Professor sits on her high log, and Vishna sits on the ground and wraps her skirt round her legs, and hugs her knees, and listens, and asks questions. I do not understand what they are talking about, but I love the words and I think about the colours, sparkling in the air as they talk, flashing backwards and forwards between them, painting the air with purples and blues, violets and pinks, and deep, dark black.

Vishna looks at me during one of those conversations and says, "What are you thinking about, Giorgio?"

And I say, "The colours."

She says, looking confused, "Which colours?"

I do not usually talk about the colours of words. I used to think everyone saw them, but when Skye discovered what I was talking about, when I was still very little, she explained that words do not have colours for lots of people. This is something I cannot quite imagine, but I asked Little Bear once what he thought was the colour of the word *bread,* and he said, "It depends whether it is brown bread or white bread, and whether it has gone mouldy!"

Then I knew that Little Bear does not see colours like me, because the word *bread* is a beige colour whatever the actual colour of the bread in real life.

So I say, "In my head, words have colours. I like them."

Vishna looks at the Professor with a worried look on her face. She thinks there is something wrong with me. The Professor says, "Synaesthesia! Perfectly normal! Nothing to worry about!"

Then to me she says, "Consider it a gift, young Giorgio. Treasure it."

★ ★ ★

Vishna and the Professor do not ignore me. If Vishna is making tea, she always offers me a mug too. If they hear Walking Tall calling us to classes they say, at once, "Off you go, Giorgio!" They always know I am there.

But they do not bother me. I have a knife which Spanner-

69

in-the-Works gave me, and I am carving a small totem pole to help make it pour and fill up the paddling pool. I carve and listen, and watch the colours in my head. Sometimes I hear the Music Maker singing in the woods, and I notice that the trees are turning to brown and gold, and I feel that I am happy, even though Skye is not there. When Music Maker sings his *But you're not there* song I try to send messages in the air to keep Skye safe.

One day the Professor says, "How's the research going, young man?"

I have not done any for several days, since Skye left. I say, "Slowly."

She says, "Not at all, I think!"

Then she says, "I always used to tell my students, you start off keen and then somewhere down the road you lose your enthusiasm. It happens to most people. That is when you have to start on the real graft. That's where half my higher degree students failed."

Vishna says, "Where did you teach, Professor?"

The Professor says, "Here." Then she waves her hand across the valley to the other side, where the old prison is (not the new, private enterprise prison called *Greenhill Reformatory*), and she says, "At the university."

"Was it good?" asks Vishna.

"For years it was wonderful," says the Professor. "We were only a small university, by most standards, but we were going up in the world. I loved teaching. All those bright, young minds! And my colleagues – you could not ask for a more interesting bunch of people, although none of us were really first in our fields."

"Then what?" I ask, because obviously something went wrong, or the Professor would not be sitting on a tall log by a fireplace on the Hill, with us.

The Professor sighs. "Well, Giorgio," she says, "it's the

same old story. The university has connections with the church. The church has connections with the government. The government has connections with the Americans. And the Americans did not like what I was teaching."

She sighs, and says again, "No, they *really* did not like what I was teaching!"

"So what happened?" asks Vishna.

For a few minutes the Professor is quiet. Then, "To cut a long story short," she says, "I heard on the grapevine that I was going to be called in for questioning. So I packed my bags and went to the nature reserve. We were raided, but I got away, and I ended up here."

I could not imagine the Professor fleeing into the nature reserve, hobbling with her stick and her briefcase filled with books. I say, "Wow!"

The Professor chuckles and says, "Oh, I was younger then!"

★ ★ ★

After this the Professor says she wants to help me with my research. She says, "Aren't you supposed to ask everyone in the camp? You haven't asked me!"

"Sorry, Professor," I say, and I am, because I really like her and I do not think she is at all scary anymore, and I do not want her to feel left out. "Can you tell me about a George I don't already have in my notebook?"

"I can do better than that!" she says, "I can tell you about a *Giorgio* you don't have in your notebook!"

I am very interested. "An Italian?" I ask, because I have learnt from Vishna that Giorgio is an Italian name.

"Yes, indeed," says the Professor.

Vishna says quietly, "I'll make tea," which really means, *I'll leave you two to it, without interrupting.*

The Professor smiles at Vishna and then says to me, "He was a very special guy, Giorgio Chiarelli. He was Jewish, and he lived in Italy during the Second World War. Do you know about the Second World War?"

"A bit," I say. "Nazis and concentration camps. And the Americans helped us but they left us with a huge debt, and we didn't finish paying it off until the beginning of this century."

"Huh!" says the Professor. "An interesting collection of some of the bare bones!"

"Right," she continues. "So, Giorgio Chiarelli came from the south of Italy, but he was living in Venice in the area called the ghetto when war broke out. He was Jewish, and Italy was friendly with Germany, so things did not look good for him."

"They would have called him in for questioning," I say, "like they did you."

"Mm," says the Professor. "Well, let's hope it's not quite the same! But yes, you get the picture. All the Jews in the ghetto area were arrested, and many went to concentration camps and died there, but Giorgio Chiarelli was kept in a camp called Fossoli, and not deported. And he wrote the most amazing poems while he was there. They released him a day after Benito Mussolini was ousted."

"Ousted?" I query, because it is a new word.

"Turfed out," says Vishna, handing the Professor some of her special tea. Then she adds, "Mussolini was Hitler's friend."

She hands me mint tea, and sits down again to listen.

I ask, "Was Giorgio Chiarelli a good man, a bad man or a gifted man?"

"What interesting categories!" says the Professor. "Are all your Georges one of those three?"

"Uh-ha," I say.

The Professor says, "Well, there's a different topic for

consideration! I would say that he was a gifted man – very gifted – but also a good man."

"Why was he good?" I want to know.

"Because he was against bad things. He was against Hitler and Mussolini, and putting people in concentration camps. And when he was in the camp called Fossoli he made a school for children, and he gave away his food, so that it is surprising that he made it out alive. But he was gifted too."

"Did he design things?" I ask, thinking of my other Giorgio.

Vishna chuckles. The Professor says, "No, he wrote things. Novels and poems." The she starts to recite, in English, *"Here the children cry, for love and joy in darkened times, and justice cries with them..."* Then she says, "That's the children of the poor today."

I think about being lost outside the supermarket, and Skye finding me crying, and care homes and labour camps, and I see that we, too, live in darkened times. So I say, "I think perhaps my parents named me after Giorgio Chiarelli."

"I think it's quite likely," says the Professor. "Who else would they name you after?"

★ ★ ★

Spanner-in-the-Works comes up the Hill when the shadows are already quite long, and he has a bin bag over his shoulder, which looks heavy. He puts it down carefully by Walking Tall's fire and starts to sing, quite loudly, *"Oranges and lemons, say the bells of St Clements."*

We all drop what we are doing and go to see what he has got. Inside the bin bag is a big pile of oranges and bananas, also a couple of onions and a rather bendy-looking cucumber.

Everyone makes pleased sounds, like:

"Great!"

Or, "Wow!"

Or, "That's a bit of a windfall!"

Or, "How come?"

Spanner-in-the-Works is looking very pleased with himself. "I was sitting in the multi-storey," he says, "talking to some blokes." We all know that the blokes in the multi-storey are not yet feckless, officially, but they use drugs and drink alcohol out of old water bottles. Spanner-in-the-Works used to hang out with those guys until he became totally feckless and came to live with us.

"Were you drinking?" asks Vishna, who also used to know those blokes in her student days.

"What the eyes don't see…" says Spanner-in-the-Works, which I am pretty sure means Yes!

Then he says, "Anyhow, there we were, on deck three, when this Salvation Army girl comes over and says, 'They're giving away free fruit on the market.' So me and a couple of the blokes go down there to look, and the stallholder gives us these!"

"Just like that?" Everyone is amazed.

"Well, he asked me questions, like 'Are you homeless?' and 'Do you have homeless friends?' And I said I knew some kids who were homeless, and he gave me this lot."

By now the Professor has hobbled over. She picks up one of the oranges and squeezes it. "Nice and fresh," she says.

"But why did he give you these?" Little Bear asks.

"Did you tell him where we live?" Big Bear wants to know, looking concerned.

"I told him nothing," says Spanner-in-the-Works. "And I think he gave us this fruit because he is a good bloke. And because it is the end of the day and nobody else was wanting to buy anything." Then he adds, "He gave stuff away to lots of people. Well, several."

Then we divide up the food and people take their shares back to their fireplaces ready to make dinner.

★ ★ ★

The next day it is drizzling. I wear my waterproof jacket and my flip-flops, but my feet are cold, and soon, I know, we will all have to wear some sort of shoes, even around the camp. Still, I am in a good mood. We had fresh orange juice for breakfast, thanks to the market man, and bread with cheese. I do not know where the cheese came from.

Then I go up the Hill to see the Old Man. He is waiting for me, and that also makes me feel good.

He does not say anything, just waves his hand towards the logs, to tell me to sit down, and holds his hand out for my research book. I hand it over, feeling proud. I have asked everyone in the camp about Georges and, although the kids were not much help at all, all the grown-ups have told me something. I have made notes about the famous Georges and the bad ones, but when people have just told me about a friend, or an uncle, then I have put them on a separate list, because although those Georges were important to the people who knew them, I do not think my mum and dad would have named me after them.

The Old Man passes me my tea and starts looking at my notebook very carefully. He reads every page, even the pages he has read before, and sometimes he turns back and rereads something more than once.

After quite a long time he says, "This is excellent, Giorgio. Well done!"

I am feeling pleased. Then he says, "Some of your English needs a bit of work. Ask the Professor to teach you about apostrophes."

Apostrophes is an amazing word, full of colours and shapes.

It is an exciting word, and I think I will enjoy learning about these things.

"And you still muddle up *there* and *their*," he says. "But you usually get it right, so I expect that's just a matter of proofreading."

He passes me back the notebook. "So, what are you going to do with all this now?" he asks.

"We're doing presentations," I tell him. "Next week. To everyone – the kids and the adults too. Will you come?"

"Yes, indeed!" says the Old Man. "In fact, you are all coming up here, to me, for that. We're going to make a party of it." Then I remember that the Old Man never comes down to the camp, so if we want him to hear what we have to say, of course we will have to come to him.

The Old Man smiles to himself. Then he says, "Yes, indeed. A party!"

I do not say anything, because I have a feeling the Old Man is not ready for me to go away. We listen to the birds, and to a bumble bee buzzing in some fireweed that grows where the sun comes through the trees.

After a while the Old Man says, "What started you on all this, Giorgio? Remind me."

I am sure he does not need reminding. I think it is me who needs to remember how it started.

I say, "I wanted to know why I am called *Giorgio*. Skye said my mum and dad might have called me after someone important, or someone in my family."

"Mm," says the Old Man. "And have you been able to find the answer to that? Do you feel you know why you are called *Giorgio*?"

I look at the Old Man's billy can, because he is looking hard at me and I don't want to meet his eyes. But Skye says *honesty is the best policy* so I make myself look back at the Old Man, and I say, "No!" When I say it, I feel sad. The fact is, I

76

started out looking for clues so that I could find my parents, and I have found out lots of interesting things, but I am no closer to finding my mum and dad.

"That's what I thought," says the Old Man.

He sits forward on his log, so that he is sort of leaning towards me. It makes me feel as if he is about to say something very important. He says, "Giorgio, do you know what a *working hypothesis* is?"

I say, "Well, I know what *working* is. What's a hyp… hyp…" I have forgotten the rest of the word, although I know it is purple.

The Old Man says, "Well, a hypothesis is like an educated guess. So, a working hypothesis is an educated guess that we will work with for now, although in the future we might find that our educated guess was wrong."

I nod.

The Old Man says, "I think you need to form a working hypothesis about why you are called *Giorgio.*"

Oh," I say, "I see."

I think the Old Man is going to help me, but he is not. He says, "Talk to Vishna about it. Or the Professor." Then he says, "I'll see you at the presentation," so I know that the Old Man has finished helping me with my research.

★ ★ ★

After our classes, which are all to do with the atlas, I tell Vishna and the Professor about the working hypothesis.

Vishna says, "That's quite a hard thing for a small boy to do."

But the Professor says, "Nonsense! The boy's got a good head on his shoulders! We'll lick this in no time, won't we, Giorgio?"

I say, "Yes," although I am not as confident as she is.

Then it seems that the Professor plans to start at once. She says, "Let's start with what we know for sure. Which country does your name come from?"

"Probably Italy," I say.

"And does that mean your parents were Italian?"

I nearly say, Yes, but in time I realise that of course it means no such thing. Conner's name is Irish but he comes from a poor city in England. Liverpool, I think. It is why he has a funny accent. So I say, "No, not necessarily."

"Good!" says the Professor, as if I have just said something really clever. "But it probably means your family had some connection with Italy."

"Yes," I agree.

"Well, that was the easy part!" says the Professor. "Now, what do we know about where you were found?"

"Skye found me in the supermarket car park," I remind her.

"And what sort of people leave their children in supermarket car parks, instead of taking them into the shop?"

Vishna says, "Professor, he won't know that. People don't do it anymore."

"Oh dear! No! Nor they do," says the Professor. "How time passes!" Then she says, "Well, a few years back people didn't glean in the night-time as much as we do now. They used to go to supermarkets at the end of the day to see if they could buy food that was going off, or even steal things. But they never took their children in, in case there were police or social workers there, and they were questioned about their ability to care for their kids. So they left them outside."

"So my mum and dad were poor," I say, following her argument.

"Exactly!" says the Professor. "Now, if they were poor, I don't suppose they would have been fans of the George Bushes, so you can rule them out."

Vishna says, "Professor, are you sure that's right? I thought quite a lot of poor people liked them?"

The Professor says, "Not in this country! And we're just forming a working hypothesis here. We'll stick with this."

"Okay," says Vishna.

"Now," says the Professor, "there is something else we know about your parents. We know they were clever."

"How do you know that?" I wonder.

"Well," says the Professor, "at least some of our brain power is inherited. We get it from our ancestors. You are a bright little chap, so I think we can assume that your parents were bright too."

Vishna says, "That's clever." I agree with her, but I don't say anything.

"So, Giorgio," says the Professor, "if your parents were bright but poor, what does that tell us?"

"That they were feckless?" I suggest.

"Oh, I don't think so!" says the Professor. "I think it means they were people who questioned things. People who thought for themselves. Perhaps the authorities said they were feckless, but then, they'll say that about anyone! I'm sure they say that about me, if they think I'm still alive!"

Vishna understands where all this is going before I do. "So, you think that Giorgio's parents will have admired a George who thought for himself?" she suggests.

"Got it in one!" says the Professor, sounding excited. "So now, Giorgio, look through your research and tell me about someone that intelligent, free-thinking people might admire."

I start to look through my list. I am feeling quite excited. We are doing a real bit of detective work. I say, "George Harrison!"

Vishna says, "That's just what I was thinking!"

The Professor says to Vishna, "I told you this exercise would not be too difficult for the boy!"

Then to me she says, "So, our working hypothesis is this: one or more of your ancestors came to England, in the days when it was easy for Europeans to come here, from Italy. Your parents were bright and educated people and they admired George Harrison. Perhaps one of his songs was especially important to them, or maybe they just respected his spiritual journey. So they called you *Giorgio* for your Italian ancestry and for George Harrison."

Vishna hugs me. "Wow!" she says, "Now you've got something to live up to!" And I feel proud, and wish that Skye would come home soon so that I can tell her.

CHAPTER 3

The Sign

I have not told you about the People who the Old Man says must be saints. It is like the gleaning. There are things the grown-ups do which they prefer us to stay out of, for our own well-being. They do not like us to go into the city at night to filch stuff which people have thrown out, and they generally try to keep us away from the People, even though they must be saints and have only ever done good by us. I went gleaning once with Skye when I was little, the time I lost my solar-powered toy, but that was because I was very small, and had a cold, and cried every time she tried to leave me behind. And it was because we were all hungry on the Hill, and we were short of people who dared go into the city, what with probation orders and Prices on their Heads. I do not remember much about the gleaning, only that we all felt frightened, and had to hide from the police in the little alleyway by the fish and chip restaurant.

I am quite excited today because Sputnik and Spanner-in-the-Works are letting me help pick up the food from the People. They really wanted Big Bear to help them. Big Bear is growing tall and strong, and has hair growing in his armpits, and will soon be a man, old enough to go to a labour camp, or to prison. But Big Bear has hurt his shoulder, and Walking Tall says it is better if he rests it up for a day or two.

So I say, "Can I help?"

I think they will all say no, but in fact Spanner-in-the-

Works says to Walking Tall, "What about it, mate?" and I know that if it were up to him, he would say yes.

Then Walking Tall, who is in charge of me when Skye is away, because I sleep in his shelter, says to me, "You will be careful, won't you, Giorgio? And quiet?"

"Yes!" I say, and I feel very grown up.

I do not know how it came about that the People Who Must Be Saints started to help us. I think maybe it was before I came to the Hill, or maybe I was already here and I was too little to notice. In the old days, they used to bring billy cans of soup and properly cut sandwiches, as well as the water, and Skye says the water used to come in plastic bottles but now it comes in glass, with a label telling the drinker that he or she can get ten cents back if they return the bottle. The deal is, though, that we give the bottles back to the People. It is only fair. They buy the water in the first place, so the ten cents are really theirs.

Nowadays they do not bring us soup or fresh-cut sandwiches anymore. I hear the Music Maker saying to Walking Tall, "I think things must be pretty tough for them, too." They bring us water and packets of crisps, and cereal bars sometimes, and sometimes fish, called *sardines*, in tins.

"They're doing the best they can," says Walking Tall

And the Music Maker adds, "Well, it's a heck of a lot more than most people do!"

The People always come at night, so that the police and the anti-terrorists, who Spanner-in-the-Works says are the scourge of the nation, do not catch them. If they are caught they will be labelled anti-social, and although they will not go straight to a labour camp, or to prison, the way we would, Skye says it would be the first step on the slippery slope.

Sputnik and Spanner-in-the-Works wear trainers down the Hill because they make for quiet walking, and because they are carrying the empty water crates and need to be sure-footed. I only have one pair of shoes and my flip-flops, and both make a lot of noise, and anyhow I am better in bare feet. We start off walking in quite an ordinary way, but we turn off our usual track and after that we do not talk anymore. It is quite late, but not very late. The street lights in the city turn themselves off at midnight, but it is only just after eleven. We hear the cathedral clock chime on our way down, and then a small, tinny striking from the clock that only works half the time, in the shopping centre.

Sputnik whispers very quietly into my ear, "We will wait here, Giorgio, to check that it's really them."

I understand that it will be a disaster if the police or the anti-terrorists figure out what the People are doing and arrest them all, then pretend to be the People themselves, to trap us.

We wait in the darkest shadows. There are waterfowl making a noise on the riverbank and a rat scurries past us, very close, not interested in us at all, but in bits of sandwiches which daytime walkers have carelessly left lying around.

We hear a vehicle approaching, the whine of an electric engine that needs servicing, and then a dark van appears and parks in the lay-by to the old road, which is only a footpath now, and an access track.

We do not do anything. The people in the van do not do anything. Rat number two joins rat number one and they squeak, which is not a noise I like. There is a gentle ripple on the river. Still nothing happens.

At last Spanner-in-the-Works says to Sputnik, very quietly, more like a breath than a whisper, "Seems okay."

"Yup," whispers Sputnik. "Let's go for it."

Then Sputnik and Spanner-in-the-Works step out into the silent moonlight and I follow them, because they do not tell me not to. The doors of the van open and two people get out. They do not look at us, just go to the back of the van and take out two crates of bottled water and three big boxes.

Sputnik picks up the boxes in turn, to see how heavy they are, and gives me one to carry. It is bigger but not as heavy as the others. Spanner-in-the-Works hides the crates of water in the dark place where we were waiting. He will have to make a second trip to carry it all up the Hill.

"Thanks, mate," says Spanner-in-the-Works, and one of the People says, "You're welcome!"

Then they get into their van and drive away.

We open the boxes when we are safely home, and while Spanner-in-the-Works is fetching the second crate of water. There are sardines in the really heavy box, and crisps in the big, light box which I brought up the Hill. We expect to find cereal bars in the third box but when we open it, it is packed to the brim with chocolate bars in different coloured wrappers.

"Oh, my goodness!" says Little Bear's mum. "The kids'll be in seventh heaven tomorrow!"

I go to bed. They let me have one of the chocolate bars to say *thank you* for my sterling efforts. I unwrap it and eat it when I am in my sleeping bag, next to Little Bear who has his head right under the covers, as he often does. The chocolate bar is full of something sweet and sticky, and it is delicious although my teeth feel gummy after I have eaten it. I think to myself, *I'm already in seventh heaven!* Then I start to wonder about the first six heavens. If chocolate bars are in the seventh heaven, what are in the first six?

★ ★ ★

Vishna and I go into the city the day Skye comes back, so by mistake I am not there to see her return. Walking Tall thinks I am in pretty good hands with Vishna, because she knows the ropes and can easily pass for someone who is a respectable citizen, as long as she covers up her tattoo.

"Why did you get a tattoo?" I ask her as we slither down

the Hill. The path is wet this morning. We are carrying our shoes, so as not to make them muddy. We will wash our feet in the river at the bottom.

"To spite my parents," says Vishna.

"Why did you want to spite your parents?" I wonder. I am thinking that if I had parents I would want to make them happy, not spite them.

"Well, you know…" says Vishna. And that is that.

★ ★ ★

We are going to see the man at the fruit stall. He has told us we may come at any time, because he will always have something for us. "Perfectly good grub," he says, meaning food, "but the likes of this lot won't pay a dime for it if a wasp or a caterpillar has so much as looked at it."

"What about the JAMS?" I ask. Surely, I think, people who are just about making it would buy apples or cabbages with small marks on them?

"Huh!" says the man. "They used to come here at the end of the day, and pay a few cents for whatever they needed, until the government switched to giving them food stamps, which they can only use in certain shops. But some of them come by here, and then I help them."

Today it is a Tuesday. We go to the stall, carrying our shopping bag, as usual. My feet are still a little squelchy from washing them in the river but I am quite smartly turned out, with my hair combed.

The market man sees us, and says, "Morning, you two!"

Then he looks worried. "Shouldn't young Sonny Jim be in school? They all went back last week."

By *Sonny Jim* he means me.

Uh-ho! Vishna and I both see that we have a problem. We are sure that the man knows I do not go to school, he knows perfectly well that we are feckless, and Scum of the Earth, but he is warning us that I will stand out, because no law-abiding citizen would be wandering around the city with a school-age child like me.

Vishna is quick off the mark. "Dental appointment," she says, and the man hands back our shopping bag, full of fruit and vegetables that caterpillars and wasps have just barely looked at.

"Is that so?" says the man. To me he says, "Nothing too painful, I hope?" Then he says to Vishna. "Better get him back to the classroom. You don't want people asking questions."

We say, "Thank you," and Vishna says, "I will!" and we walk back down the High Street.

★ ★ ★

After a few yards, Vishna says, "That's a pain."

"Yes," I say, thinking that I will not be able to come down into the city with Vishna anymore, except at weekends.

"Sit here a minute," says Vishna, and we sit on a bench looking towards the Guildhall. Two people walk past us very slowly, a man and a woman in smart clothes with labels on bits of tape round their necks. They give Vishna and me a long, thoughtful look, but they do not stop and talk to us.

Vishna says quite loudly, "We'll go back to school when the anaesthetic has worn off, Edward."

Edward? That is clever of Vishna, I think. So I say, also a little more loudly than I would normally talk, "All right, Mary."

As soon as the man and woman are out of earshot, Vishna says, "School attendance officers."

"What are they?" I want to know.

"Social workers," says Vishna. "We'd better scram."

We start walking down the street again. We are going to

cross the Abbey Gardens and go past the cathedral and then the Bishop's Palace, on our way home.

Only I have a really uncomfortable feeling. I look behind me, and there is a policeman typing into his droid. Then Vishna says, "Oh dear!" The two school attendance officers have turned around and are coming back towards us. Fortunately, they are both looking at their devices.

"Quick!" says Vishna, and grabs me by my sweatshirt and pulls me into the nearest doorway.

We are in a little church. I think it is very old, with stone arches and a table covered with a cloth.

And on the cloth is a cross, without a man stuck to it. A cross like the cross in the Q of my necklace.

"Hey, Vishna, look!" I say, and I go over and pick up the cross. It is large and heavy, and very shiny.

Vishna has closed the church door. Now we are seeing everything by the light of two dim electric lamps made to look like candles, which are by the table. She sees me holding the cross, and says, "I don't think you should touch that, Giorgio."

I put it back. "Why?" I want to know.

"Well, it's sort of holy," she says. "And anyhow, if anyone came in they would think you were nicking it."

I can see that she is right. Vishna is sitting on one of the long wooden benches. I sit next to her.

"Why is it holy?" I want to know.

"Don't you know anything about churches?" asks Vishna. She is not being critical, she is just interested.

"Not really." Then I think I need to explain. "Religion causes a lot of trouble," I tell her. "It's best to keep away from it."

"Well, yes…" says Vishna. "I suppose it's like everything. It does some good and some harm."

I remember something I have been told. "When Dragon's

Child was in care it was a religious place, and they hit her a lot."

"Oh," says Vishna. Then she says, "I think the People who bring us the water are religious."

Now I am getting quite muddled. "But they are doing a good thing," I point out. "The Old Man says they might be saints."

Vishna goes across to the table where the cross is. "Haven't you noticed?" she asks. "You see this sign everywhere."

I have not noticed, but I am interested. "Is the cross a sign or a thing?"

Vishna picks it up, despite the fact that it is holy, then puts it gently down again. "I think it is a sign *and* a thing," she says. "You ought to get Skye or someone to tell you about it. There's a good story which goes with it."

She goes to the door of the church and opens it a little. The outside looks very bright after the dim light of the inside. She says, "It's safe!"

On the way home, we see how many crosses we can see. There are quite a few on and around the cathedral, but other than them we do not see too many at all. I think Vishna is exaggerating when she says you see the cross everywhere. Nevertheless, it has been an interesting morning. I think that if we do another bit of research I will investigate crosses.

★ ★ ★

When we get home, Skye is there. She has brought back a winter gilet for me. It is padded and has a zip up the front and a pocket on the inside for keeping money and contactless cards away from pick-pockets. She has brought me a proper pair of trainers too, with military buckles, like the ones I have seen on kids in the city. And she has a pair of socks each for Little Bear and me, with cartoon characters on them.

We sit round Walking Tall's fireplace and catch up on all the news. Little Bear and I put our socks on, and laugh as the cartoon characters change shape as we pull them over our ankles.

Skye does not say much about her trip. Vishna tells her about our narrow escape with the attendance officers and everyone looks quite serious for a few minutes, thinking about what could have happened. Vishna says, "It was my fault; I should have remembered the schools have gone back."

But Skye says, "Nonsense, Vishna!" Then she adds, "It isn't getting any easier, is it? There are whole areas in the south east now, where they claim to have solved the homelessness problems altogether."

"I bet their labour camps are full!" says Sputnik, and a few people laugh, but not with happiness.

Then Skye says, "The Europeans don't like it at all."

Spanner-in-the-Works asks, "How is it their business?"

Skye answers, "Well, they have this strong commitment to human rights. People aren't locked up for being homeless in Paris or Rome or Edinburgh." Then she adds, "I need to go and talk to the Old Man."

★ ★ ★

At dinner they are all talking about this person Skye met on her travels. A captain in a religious group called the Salvation Army introduced them. It seems the Salvation Army is a group which does not cause trouble, and this captain, who Skye has known for years, thought she should meet this woman. Skye did not want to tell us about it until she had talked to the Old Man.

"She's a journalist," she says. "She works for a Swedish monthly. She wants to do an article about us."

"About *us*?" Little Bear's mum is looking worried. "How does she know anything about us?"

Walking Tall puts a hand on Little Bear's mum's arm, to calm her down.

Skye says, "She doesn't know anything about *us*. I mean she wants to write an article about the remaining homeless, about people living off the grid in England after all these years of suppression."

Spanner-in-the-Works says, "I think we ought to stay well away!"

Walking Tall says, "What does the Old Man think?"

The Professor, who has just arrived, says, "Which monthly does this journalist write for? One of my students went to work for a Swedish monthly." Then she says, "Or was it Norwegian?"

Skye says, "The Old Man thinks it might be a good thing. If the European countries put pressure on our government, our lot might tone down their actions a bit."

"Huh!" says Sputnik.

Vishna laughs.

The Professor says, "It's true. They like to think we are the leaders in opportunity and freedom. The Alliance hates it when anyone points out the inequality in our society and the faults in our penal code."

Little Bear's mum says, "I don't see how one article would make any difference."

Walking Tall answers, "I suppose it's about building up a body of opinion. People in Europe write letters to our government, you know. They sign petitions. They demonstrate outside our embassies."

"Where we still have embassies," says the Professor.

"So, what is the plan?" asks Spanner-in-the-Works.

Everyone looks at Skye. "If we all agree," she says, "I will meet this journalist and talk to her. I won't bring her up here, or tell her where we live."

Little Bear's mum says, "Everyone in the city knows we

live up here. They only leave us alone because we don't cause them any trouble."

Walking Tall says, "Perhaps it's time we *did* cause them some trouble!" Then he adds, "And anyhow, I don't think they'll let us stay up here forever. If it's true that in the south east they claim to have rid themselves of homelessness altogether, you can bet your bottom dollar Hampshire will want to follow suit. I think they'll try to close this camp down again, this winter."

Little Bear's mum says, "But we've got to be so careful. Think of the children!"

Everyone looks at Dylan, Little Bear and me, who have been sitting by the fire listening to it all, while Little Bear occasionally stirs the contents of the billy can. He sometimes cooks whole dinners on his own, now.

Walking Tall says, half to Little Bear's mum and half to the whole circle, "I've been thinking it was time we headed north, anyhow. We always knew this wouldn't last forever."

Skye says, "I might be able to help there, Walking Tall, if you're serious."

Little Bear's mum looks angrily at Skye. "Don't bother talking to me about this!" she says, and gets up and walks away.

Big Bear gets up too. He walks over to his mum, who is standing by the earthworks looking out at the city. He puts his arm round his mum's shoulders. He is taller than her now. After a few minutes they come back, and Little Bear serves us up the stew and potatoes, and we all say how good it is, and nobody says anything else about journalists or going north. But you cannot unsay things. The words which were spoken hover round the fire all evening, and their colours change the way everyone looks.

★ ★ ★

I move back to Skye's shelter at once, although her fire has not yet been lit. When she wriggles into her sleeping bag, I say, "Tell me a story about your trip, Skye."

She says, "It was just an ordinary journey, Giorgi. Just like all the others."

I say, "In this world, no two things are ever quite the same."

Skye laughs. "Where did you hear that?" she says.

"Vishna told me," I say.

Skye laughs again. "That girl is good for you!" she says. Then she adds, "And she's quite right. This time I went east, sometimes I go north, and sometimes west. But it was east this time."

"And did you meet anyone interesting?" I want to know. I really mean, *Did you meet anyone who knows about my mum and dad,* but that is not what I say. Skye told me, last time I asked, that it is extremely unlikely she will bump into them after all these years.

"I met a vicar," she says. "That's a sort of holy man."

I say, "Vishna and I went into a church. To hide. We saw a cross on a table. Vishna said it was holy."

Skye says, thoughtfully, "Well, perhaps it is, in a manner of speaking."

I say, "But doesn't religion cause a lot of trouble?"

"Mm," says Skye, who is very tired, on her side of the red partition.

"Skye," I say, "I want to do some more research, about crosses."

"Mm," says Skye again. "Ask the Old Man." She is very sleepy from walking miles and miles on her trip. She is not thinking about crosses, or holy things, or research. Almost at once she is breathing big, deep, slow breaths. She is fast asleep. I curl up too. It is good to have Skye back, and to be going to sleep in her shelter again, where I really belong.

★ ★ ★

92

Right after breakfast I head up the Hill to see the Old Man. He is tending his herb garden by the maze, and when he sees me he stands, slowly, with his hand on the small of his back.

"Oh dear!" he says, "these old bones!" Then, "I thought I might see you today. Tea?"

We sit by his fire and drink the bitter tea that is not mint. I wait for him to start.

"I think you have a question, Giorgio," he says, when our mugs are about half empty.

"I'm thinking about lots of things," I tell him. "Journalists, and people going north, and crosses."

The Old Man thinks for a bit. He says, "Well, I can see why you are wondering about journalists and going north, but where do the crosses come in?"

I say, "We saw one in a church, me and Vishna, when we were hiding from social workers. And Vishna says they are everywhere. And I want to know about them."

"Ah!" says the Old Man. "And of course, there is that necklace that came from your parents…"

"Yes," I am not surprised the Old Man knows. Skye will have told him.

"Well…" says the Old Man. There is a long pause. "More tea?" he suggests, and tops up our mugs.

We listen to the autumn leaves rustling overhead. "Soon be winter," says the Old Man, although today it is a lovely day, full of sunshine and breezes.

Then he says, "Crosses, religion, the whole business of it … Tricky, you know, Giorgio."

"Yes." I think for a bit. "Everyone is always telling me religion is dangerous," I say, "but the People Who Must Be Saints are religious, aren't they? And the Salvation Army is religious." Then I take a gamble, and I add, "And I think the Music Maker is religious, because he sings the *mighty thunder* song when he comes up here to sort out his spirit."

The Old Man chuckles. "Well done!" he says. Then he says, "You are young to be grappling with these things, Giorgio. Let me try to explain. Religion is like everything in this life – it can be good and it can be bad. On this Hill we decided to keep religion out of things, because it caused so much argument in the early days. The real trouble with religion," the Old Man sighs, "is that it is in the nature of things, that if you have a religion, you think you're right. And as often as not, you think you are doing people a favour if you convince them you're right."

I am not sure I understand. I decide I will think about what he has said later. "So, can I research crosses?" I ask the Old Man, getting back to the main point.

The Old Man looks into the bottom of his mug for a while, and I wait for him to decide. I know I will find it hard if he says no. But in fact, he looks up, and says, "I think it might be just what you need to do. Let's decide where you will start."

★ ★ ★

When I am walking down the Hill, just as I get past the trees and I am close to Walking Tall's shelter, I hear that they are having an argument.

I hear Little Bear's mum first. She is saying, "But it would be such a risk! If they caught us… The children would end up in care."

Then Walking Tall says, "My love, that is just as likely to happen if we don't go. You know the council won't let us stay here forever. I'm surprised we've got away with it for as long as we have."

Little Bear's mum sounds really, really upset. She says, "The problem is, they're not your kids. When push comes to shove, you're more concerned to get to Scotland than you are to keep the kids safe!"

I think Little Bear's mum is silly. Walking Tall is a real dad to the Bears; I heard Skye say so one night round the fire.

Walking Tall says, with a sort of tired patience in his voice, "Look, love, if Skye knows someone who can help us, it is probably the best chance we will ever have." Then he says, "We have given these kids a good life here for several years, but we're living in the present. We never know what the future will bring. If we go to Scotland we can give the kids a future, too."

Little Bear's mum says, as if she is crying, "But it's such a risk!"

I do not realise I have stopped to listen. I know it is rude to pay attention to other people's conversations. Little Bear's mum comes bursting out of the shelter. She sees me standing there. She shouts at me, "And what do you think you're doing, young man?" and rushes away round the Hill.

Walking Tall comes out after her. He sees me standing there too. I am going red in the face because Little Bear's mum yelled at me, which she has never done before. Walking Tall says, "Sorry, Giorgio. She's just upset." Then he follows her round the Hill.

I see that their fire is nearly out. They were too busying arguing to pay proper attention to it. I put some more wood on it – green wood, that will burn through slowly, and I go down to our shelter. It feels as if everything is changing.

★ ★ ★

The next time the Old Man and I talk about my cross research, he suggests I start with the Music Maker. So, after our English lesson (we are writing poems this week) and our snacks, I find him by his fire. He is talking to Big Bear about setting his poem to music. They are using words like *chords*, *harmony* and *vocals*. The Music Maker sees me standing there, and he raises one eyebrow, which means, *Well, can I help you?*

I say, "The Old Man suggested I should talk to you."

He looks a bit surprised, but not unhappy. He says to Big Bear, "So, have a go at that, and I'll see how you've got on in about an hour. Okay?"

"Yeah," says Big Bear. He is holding the Music Maker's guitar casually, as if he is very at home with it.

The Music Maker says, "Let's sit on the earthworks," and we walk down the Hill and round a bit, to the place where I suppose Walking Tall and Little Bear's mum finished their argument. Of course, they are not there now. We sit down next to each other.

The Music Maker says, "So, how can I help?"

I say, "I'm doing some more research."

"Ah-ha!" says the Music Maker. "And what would you like to know this time?"

I explain about the cross, and about the Old Man agreeing that he, Music Maker, is religious.

The Music Maker thinks for a bit. "I think we need to make a distinction," he says, "between *religion* in general, and the cross in particular."

I wait for him to explain. "As you know, I think, there are lots of different religions. George Harrison, who I told you about last time, was a Hindu. The cross is all to do with Christianity."

I half knew this. We had learnt about myths and legends, but we had kept away from beliefs because of all the trouble they can cause. The Music Maker says, "For what it's worth, Christianity is my particular religion." Then he talks for a while about Christians, and all the different types that there are in the world, and how he was once interested in becoming a priest until his eyes were opened and he felt that there was no need for priests. He says, "The thing is, Giorgio, in the end it's all between you and God. Nobody else need be involved."

It is interesting, but I think he is not helping me in my research about crosses. I say, "So, is the cross a symbol or a thing?" and hope it will bring him back to the questions I want to answer.

"Oh, both!" says the Music Maker. "There was a real cross, and a real death on the cross. No doubt about it. But it is a symbol too. It is a symbol of love."

I am a bit out of my depth. I think a heart is the symbol of love. The Music Maker says, "Jesus was a bit like us – a bit feckless. He travelled around and he mixed with all sorts of people, like we do. And he loved them all. So the cross he died on is a symbol of love."

"So, was Jesus the Scum of the Earth?" I want to know.

"Some people would certainly say so," says the Music Maker.

I think to myself that if my mum and dad had a cross in a letter Q because they were feckless, and the Scum of the Earth, then they must be people like Skye, and the Music Maker, and the Old Man. I think that perhaps, one day, they will come to the Hill, like Vishna did, and we will be reunited.

I say, "Thank you, Music Maker," and I go back to our shelter.

Further up the Hill I see that Walking Tall and Little Bear's mum are sitting by their fire. Walking Tall has his arm round Little Bear's mum's shoulder and their heads are close together. They are not arguing; you can see that even from a distance. I think they are making plans.

I think that a cross is an odd symbol for love. I think two people with their arms round each other and their heads close would be a better symbol than one man stuck on a cross, but the world is a strange place and I still have a lot to learn.

★ ★ ★

Researching the cross is not as easy as researching my name. I cannot go around the camp asking everyone if they have any special memories of crosses. In fact, other than the Music Maker and perhaps Vishna and the Professor, I am not sure I feel comfortable about raising the topic with anyone. There is another problem, too. All the grown-ups in the camp seem to be talking about the journalist from Sweden, and about the idea of going north. They are not so interested in research, and they even skip our English lesson and let us play instead, so that they can all talk about these things, round their fires and on the earthworks. Skye is looking worried. Walking Tall and Little Bear's mum go everywhere holding hands, and I see that they have reached a big conclusion, although they have not said anything to Little Bear yet.

When the grown-ups have finished talking about the journalist, I go to the Professor's fire circle, where Vishna is making a hot snack. Autumn is coming and the Professor says she can feel it in her old bones.

"This might be my last winter," she says to Vishna.

Vishna says, "Oh, I hope not," and makes a ball of dough to toast on a stick on the fire, for me.

I say, "Professor, can you tell me about crosses, please?"

"Ah, Giorgio, my boy," says the Professor. "Always asking such interesting questions! What sort of crosses are we talking about?"

"Crosses like in religion," I say. "Crosses round people's necks and crosses in churches."

"My goodness!" says the Professor. "You're not turning all religious, are you? I never had much time for religion, myself, although I appreciate the current Archbishop of Canterbury. It takes some guts to go to prison for your faith."

I am not sure what the Professor is talking about. I see that Vishna is smiling to herself while she prepares our snacks. I am glad she does not interrupt.

I say, "I am not becoming religious, I am doing some research."

The Professor says, "Oh, in that case…"

Then she says to Vishna, "Can this young man stay to lunch? Do we have enough?"

Vishna is still smiling. She says, "We always have enough for Giorgio!"

So the Professor says, "Then you had better sit down, boy. I have quite a lot to tell you."

★ ★ ★

It is an interesting snack time. We are eating sardines from a tin the People Who Must Be Saints gave us, with little flour-and-water dough balls and spinach leaves. These are all some of my favourite foods, although it is hard to eat hot dough balls fresh from the fire without burning your fingers or your mouth.

The Professor tells me a lot of things. Some of it is quite complicated, and I am rather lost with all the history of it and the names she tells me: Martin Luther and John Calvin, the Luddites and Wycliffe, and people called popes, and the King James Bible. I do not have my notebook, and I think that a lot of this stuff is not really about crosses, but about the religion of Christianity, which is very complicated and has a long history.

When our snacks are finished and Vishna has made tea with something lemony in it, the Professor begins to slow down. I use the opportunity to ask, "And *all* these different people have crosses as their symbols?"

"That's right," agrees the Professor. "They all do, one way or another."

I can't help sighing. The cross seems to be a very complicated piece of research.

I make one more attempt to get some sense out of it all. "So why do some crosses have men stuck on them and some do not?" I want to know.

Vishna laughs, but she still does not say anything except, "More tea, Professor?"

The Professor says, "A very astute question, if I may say so, young man!"

I worry that she is going to start talking about more people I have not heard of, and do not particularly need to know about just now, but instead she gives me a really simple answer. "In the West," she says, "there are two main branches of Christianity: the Roman Catholics and the Protestants. Generally speaking, the Roman Catholics use a crucifix and the Protestants use a cross."

Although it is a short answer, I am lost again. "What's a crucifix?" I ask.

At last Vishna comes in to the conversation. "A crucifix is a cross with the statue of Jesus on it. A cross is plain."

I think of the cross in the letter Q on my necklace.

"Is it best to be Roman Catholic or Protestant?" I ask.

"Well now," says the Professor, "that is the question! But if you two young people would like to go away for a few minutes and do whatever it is young people do after lunch, I need forty winks!"

Then, without lying down, the Professor closes her eyes and her head drops forward. She is fast asleep, sitting upright on her high log.

★ ★ ★

I spend the afternoon writing down notes in my *George Pearson* notebook. I leave a couple of pages blank after the information about Georges and Giorgios, and then I write down everything useful I have found out, so far, about crosses.

There is not much to help me to find my mum and dad. The cross in the Q does not have a man stuck to it, so perhaps my parents were Protestants. I did not understand, or even listen properly, to all the Professor's talk about popes and Wycliffe and all that stuff, but I realise that I need to know which branch of the Christian religion is good and which is bad.

I go back to the Music Maker, who has reclaimed his guitar from Big Bear and is tuning it carefully.

"That boy is heavy duty!" he says to me. Then, "What's up, Giorgio?"

I plunge straight in. "When you were thinking you might be a priest," I wonder, "were you going to be a Roman Catholic or a Protestant?"

"My goodness!" says the Music Maker. "That's the strangest question a child has ever asked me!"

I think that grown-ups are not as helpful when they talk about religion as they are when they are thinking about names. "Yes, but which was it?" I ask.

The Music Maker stops tuning his guitar. He says, "Does it matter?"

I explain, "Roman Catholics have crucifixes and Protestants have crosses."

The Music Maker looks perplexed. He says, "Giorgio, I think you're barking up the wrong tree, here. The question isn't about which church you belong to, it's about what's in your heart."

He is not helping me at all. I say, "But…"

He says, looking at me quite thoughtfully, "What's this all about?"

So I tell him about the necklace I was wearing when Skye found me.

"May I see it?" the Music Maker asks gently. "Or is it too private?"

I run down the slope and go into our shelter. The little leather bag is in one of the pockets of Skye's backpack, and I pull it out and run back up to the Music Maker's fire circle.

Carefully I take it out of the bag. It lies in my hand, a silver-coloured chain with a Q and a cross inside it. I place it in the Music Maker's cupped hands. I see that it is a bit tarnished, but it still glints in the overcast light of the afternoon.

The Music Maker looks at it quietly for several minutes. Then he says, "It's lovely, Giorgio."

"Yes," I say.

Then he says, "Well, I'll be honest, I don't remember ever seeing this sign before, and I don't know what it means. But I'm sure it's special."

He passes it back to me. He says, "I used to know a lot about what was going on in the churches at one time, but this sign..." Then he adds, "The only way I would know, of finding out what it means, would be to investigate the logos of all the different churches."

"How would I do that?" I ask, looking at the little necklace nestling in my hands.

"Well, the short way would be to look on the internet," he says. "But that's easier said than done for people like us. The long way is to walk all around the city looking at every church building."

I think about that. I say, "I would be scared of social workers finding me."

"A fear that is not without justification," agrees the Music Maker.

I go back to our shelter and carefully replace the necklace

where it is safe. Then I go to find Little Bear and we play racing until dinner time.

★ ★ ★

I am busy for two days. Skye insists that we have extra lessons to make up for the ones we missed, so we have English before our snack time and again afterwards. I am learning a poem which starts *King John was not a good man...* We are all going to recite our poems, which come from a little book Vishna brought with her, to the whole group.

Little Bear says, "We might have gone by then."

"What do you mean?" I say.

Little Bear explains. I cannot tell if he is pleased or not. "We are going to go north," he tells me. "Mum and Walking Tall, and Big Bear and me. Skye is arranging it with a contact. We want to try to live in Scotland."

"You'll have to pay taxes!" I say, which has always made Little Bear laugh before. He does not laugh this time. Instead he says, "If they catch us, they'll put us in care."

I understand that this is a very serious business. I say, "Skye won't organise something that is dangerous for you."

Little Bear says, "Giorgio, *everything* is dangerous for us." He sounds sad and worried. Then he says, "Will you come with us?"

I am surprised. "Me?" I say.

Little Bear says, "If they catch us, Big Bear and Mum and Walking Tall will all go into labour camps. They're all grown up. Or even prison. If we were caught, you and me, we would both go into care and we'd be together." Little Bear fidgets, then he says very quietly, "Giorgio, I'm frightened of going into care on my own."

Little Bear is my friend. I know how he feels, too. I think about going with them all. If we got to Scotland would I count

103

as one of their family? Would I go to school, and grow up free to say what I think? But if we were caught on the way…

Then I think of my mum and dad, and the bright, golden green of my dad's word, and I think, *If I go to Scotland I might never find my parents.*

I say to Little Bear, "I don't think you'll be caught." Then I say, "I have to stay here. I have to find my mum and dad."

Little Bear says, "But…" and I think he is going to say, *there's not much chance of that!* But instead he says, "Yeah, I know."

★ ★ ★

After dinner we have a big meeting. Everyone is there. We are sitting round the Old Man's fire circle and people have brought things to share. Martha has made some cookies. Sputnik and Little Bear have made sweets out of honey and a sort of pastry. They are very sticky, and Sputnik says, "Well, what do you expect, with the wrong ingredients and the wrong temperature for cooking!" But everyone likes them, and they are gone in no time.

The grown-ups have been talking in pairs and around fire circles for two days, ever since Skye came back. Everyone has his or her own point of view. The children are either nervous, like Little Bear, or excited, like Dylan and Limpy, who are always up for adventure. I think that none of this has much to do with me because I am not going anywhere, whatever they decide.

The Old Man says, "We have two big decisions to make. Where shall we start?"

Half the adults say, "The journalist!" The other half say, "Going north!"

The Music Maker says, "If we agree to talk to the journalist we more or less have to agree to go north. Once there is an article written about us, we won't be safe here anymore."

Spanner-in-the-Works says, "Isn't it the other way around? If we decide to go north then we'll be free to talk to the journalist. If we want to stay here we can't go talking to anyone."

Walking Tall and Little Bear's mum are holding hands. Walking Tall says, "I don't know if this is relevant, but we're going north anyhow. Soon. We need to give our kids a future."

Everyone looks at Walking Tall. Little Bear, who is sitting with them, shuffles his bare feet in the leaves that have started to fall. He does not look across the circle to me.

Sputnik says, "Wow!"

Martha says, "Well, I would do the same in your place. In fact…"

Firefly's mum says, "There isn't really a future for our kids here."

Scott, who has a girlfriend in the city, asks, "How big a risk is it, going north? I mean…"

Everyone looks at Skye. She says, "Well, of course it *is* a risk, but quite a lot of people have done it. There's an escape route that is working quite well just now, and more sympathy for us in Scotland than there used to be." Then she says, "In Kent and Buckinghamshire the number of kids in care has rocketed. We have to think about that, too."

We all know what she means. If we stay here we are running big risks, so it is a question of balancing one risk against another.

Firefly's mum says, "I'm for going north."

Florence, Limpy's mum, says, "Would Limpy's bad leg be a problem? On the journey, I mean?"

Skye says reassuringly, "No, I don't think so."

The Old Man says, "It is beginning to sound as if people favour going north."

All round the circle people say:

105

"Yes,"

"It looks like it."

"Well, we want to go north."

And, "Do we really have a choice?"

The Old Man asks, "Is there anyone who does *not* want to leave here?"

The Professor says, "Well, I'm way past going anywhere. I'll stay here until the Grim Reaper comes to claim me!"

And I say, "I'll stay here too. I need to find my mum and dad."

The circle goes quiet. Skye holds my hand, and in the colours of all the talking we have done I think I see the bright green-gold of my dad.

★ ★ ★

After that there is a whole lot of serious discussion. People want Skye to tell them about the escape route which is working pretty well just now, but although she is very reassuring she does not actually answer anyone's questions. It seems nearly everyone intends to go. Scott says he will talk his girlfriend into it, because although she is not feckless, and has a job, and lives in a house with her mum and dad, there is no future for them as a couple if they stay here. Martha wants to know if she can contact her sister, who got out of a labour camp a few months ago, and lives in a halfway house and picks watercress for a pittance. People ask questions about travelling together, and about papers, and about the cost of all this, and remember terrible stories they heard once about people smugglers.

Skye listens to it all, but she just says, to comfort everyone, "I don't have anything to do with people smugglers. My contacts have better motives than that!"

It is only late in the evening, when children are asleep

on the laps of parents, or lying on their tummies facing the fire, and poking it lazily with sticks, that the grown-ups talk about the journalist. Now that they have decided to go north, nobody cares too much about this Swedish writer. She will want to write about our camp, but the days of our camp are nearly over.

★ ★ ★

I am sure that Skye will want me to think again about my decision not to go north. I am half expecting her to say something when, after midnight, with all the city blacked out in the valley below us, we finally stop talking and go back to our shelters. But she just says, "Sweet dreams, Giorgio," and ruffles my hair.

Next morning the Professor comes to our fireplace while I am still eating bread. Skye has cut the green bits off, and I am toasting it because then it tastes better. The Professor has her usual stick, and a second, long piece of wood I have not seen before, to keep her steady. She sits down without asking, and sighs.

"It's all very well," she says, to no one in particular, "living on the side of a hill in the summer, when the grass is dry, but my feet can't keep their grip in all this damp autumn weather."

I am bare-footed, but I have not noticed how heavy the dew is until now. Perhaps it even rained a little in the night. I go around without shoes so much that my feet do not notice things like wet grass or small stones. The Professor always wears shoes.

Skye says, "All the more reason for coming north with the rest of us."

The Professor says, "No! No! If I had been going to do that, I would have done it years ago. I'll just stay here and face whatever is coming my way."

Then she says to me, "And are you going to stay and keep me company, young man?"

I look at Skye. I say, "Skye wants me to go north, and Little Bear wants me to travel with them…"

Skye says, "I haven't said that, Giorgi."

"No," I say, "but I know."

Skye is washing up mugs in a little dribble of water. She sits down again, next to me, and says, "I never, ever want to make you do something against your will, Giorgi, but have you really thought about this? How will you live if we are all gone? I will worry about you every day."

I practise picking up a stick with my toes, so that I do not have to look at her. I do not want to make Skye worry every day, but I do not want to leave Winchester.

The Professor says, "She has a point, Giorgio."

I try picking up sticks with my other foot. My left toes are not as clever as my right toes.

The Professor says to Skye, "Should I go? Leave you to talk to our Giorgio alone?"

Skye thinks for a moment, and says, "It makes no difference. Giorgi has a mind of his own. If he wants to stay…"

I say, "I really want to find my mum and dad!"

Skye puts her hand on my arm and says sadly, "I know. I do know that. But you know, Giorgi, it's already years since you came to live here. They could be anywhere."

The Professor says, sounding suddenly bright, "Many years ago, when I lived over there…" she waves across the misty valley to the university buildings by the old prison, "there used to be a television programme. They would trace people's long-lost families and put them back in touch again. It was a very popular series." Then she says, sounding a little disgruntled for a moment, "Very emotional, I seem to remember." Then her grumpiness goes again. "Perhaps they have programmes like that in Scotland, Giorgi. Perhaps they would be able to find your family."

I look at the Professor. I see that she means well, but I do not think a Scottish television company will want to help me find my mum and dad. I look at Skye. She has wrinkled up her forehead, because she is thinking hard. She says, "Giorgi, if you're really set on staying, maybe I can fix something up for you. You're too young to be left on your own. And I'll come back and check on you, whenever I can."

"That's the ticket!" says the Professor.

★ ★ ★

After maths, I say to Spanner-in-the-Works, "How can I look something up on the internet?"

Spanner-in-the-Works says, "The short answer to that, Giorgi my boy, is that you can't!"

"But I really need to," I say.

He stops what he is doing. They are all making bags or sacks for carrying their stuff north. Every bag has to be waterproof and small enough for the owner to carry all day. They can only take the minimum of stuff.

He says, "The thing is, Giorgi, our government does not much want people like us finding out things, or contacting each other privately. There was a time when it was easy, what with encryption and data roaming, but they've more or less put a stop to that now."

I do not know what these things are, but I ask, "Can people who aren't feckless look at the internet?"

"They can," says Spanner-in-the-Works. "But the anti-terrorists are always spying on them, to see what they're up to."

I ask, "So, how would a boy who is not feckless look something up? If he was doing research for school?"

Spanner-in-the-Works thinks about this. "Schools all have droids," he says, "and kids have them at home. And there are devices in libraries. But none of them are secret from the anti-terrorists."

"Thank you," I say, and wander back to our fireplace. I am trying to think whether the anti-terrorists would mind a boy looking up religious symbols. I think it seems like quite harmless research.

There is a library in the city. It is run by volunteers, and I saw a notice that said children under ten can use it for free.

I say to Big Bear, who is strumming the Music Maker's guitar, "Do you think I'm under ten, Big Bear?"

He looks me up and down. "Yea," he says, "you're a little squirt of a kid!" He is teasing me, but I have got my answer.

★ ★ ★

The journalist wants to meet Skye in a coffee shop in the city. Skye thinks it is funny. "Does she really think," she asks Walking Tall and Little Bear's mum, "that I could sit and talk to her, about all this, in public, in a coffee shop in Winchester?"

Little Bear's mum says, "So what did you say?"

"I suggested the nature reserve," she says. "I know pretty much all the ways in and out of there, if need be, and it's not such an odd thing, to suggest a walk by the river on a beautiful autumn day."

"Well, good luck to you," says Little Bear's mum. Now that they know for sure that they are going, she is much happier and more relaxed, and she holds Walking Tall's hand a lot, and smiles at me as if she has never shouted at me for listening to their row.

I say, "Skye, can I come? I've never met a journalist."

Skye laughs. "Not this time," she says, as if there might

be lots of other opportunities in the future, journalists just queuing up in coffee shops and nature reserves all around the country wanting to talk to me.

So I decide to follow her. Everyone else is making preparations, and there is nobody to play with.

★ ★ ★

We used to camp in the nature reserve, years ago, when the police used to raid the Hill. It is a huge, flat area very close to the river, and it floods a lot, and foxes live there and swans nest besides the paths. It is called *Winnall Moors*. We used to go as far upriver as we could, beyond the part where walkers and joggers go. It was never as safe as the Hill. We were not allowed to play noisy games there. It was just a place to hide.

I do not follow Skye down the Hill. I know where she is going anyhow, and I think she is quite good at noticing if somebody is keeping an eye on her. I take the long, back path down to the road. Then I put my new socks and trainers on and comb my hair, and try to look as if I am not at all feckless, and I just walk along the road, past houses and cars and people walking dogs, until I get to the little bridge where the feeding station used to be. One of the ways into the nature reserve is there.

A man is standing by the wooden arch which is the entry. He is wearing a badge which says *Volunteer*. He does not look very happy, and I wonder why he volunteers to work there if he does not enjoy it. When he sees me, he says, "Hurry up! Hurry up! All the others are at the hide. Take the left path and then turn right. You can't miss them!" Under his breath he says, "Making enough noise to wake the dead. Frightening away every living creature for miles!"

I do not know where Skye and the journalist plan to meet. There are benches all around this end of the nature reserve, and they could be anywhere. I plan to walk once round the edge, the way most people seem to go. Beyond the gate in the north end is the area where we used to hide, but it is wilder there and not so many people want to go that far.

I start to follow the path, and I see at once why the volunteer was so grumpy. There is a crowd of boys, whooping and yelling. A woman is in charge of them. She is saying, "Now then, boys!" and, "That's enough, please!" and they are paying no attention at all.

Then I see the greenish-grey jacket that Skye wears, and a tall woman walking beside her, wearing smart boots almost up to her knees, and a swishy skirt. I hide in the reeds behind them and pretend I am an anti-terrorist spy and I am going to catch them in the act.

Skye and the journalist sit on a bench made of carved wood, looking across at the art school. The journalist has one of those devices you talk into, which the police use, and she also writes notes on a piece of paper. I think she has a hoody on under her coat, the way some people dress in the winter, and it is surprising at this time of the year. I can picture where Sweden is on the map in our atlas, and it is north of England, and colder I think. So why is the journalist dressed like that now? Every now and again, Skye points at something, and sometimes they both laugh. I am not close enough to hear what they are saying.

After a while I get bored. There was so much discussion about the risks of talking to a journalist, and how it could not be done in a coffee shop, and how it would have been the end of our camp if they had not decided already to go north, that somehow I thought it would be more dramatic than this. It is just two women sitting on a bench talking, one scruffy and one very smart, with her hood up.

I decide that I will go back to the Hill, but first I want to see if I can find any living creatures. I follow the path around the other way, away from Skye and the journalist, and look besides the track, where once Dylan and I found tiny, green frogs wanting to cross from one side to the other.

I do not see any; I think it must be the wrong time of year. So I am about to give up when I notice that Skye and the journalist have finished talking. Skye is walking slowly towards the exit, looking relaxed, like a person who is not feckless, going for a stroll. The journalist continues to sit on the bench. She is looking through her notes and switching the recording device on and off. I think she is checking to see that everything Skye said is safely stored. I decide that I will spy on her a little bit more, before I go back to the Hill.

There is no path behind the bench, just the reeds where I was hiding a few minutes ago, and some very boggy ground. It is a pity I am wearing good trainers and socks because I have made them really dirty with black mud, but the harm has already been done. I creep up behind the journalist. She does not seem to hear me, and I am very quiet. I pretend I am an anti-terrorist man about to capture someone who is a threat to civilisation as we know it, and I think I will creep right up behind her.

About ten feet away from her I think I have done enough. The woman is sitting very still, not looking at her droid or notes, staring at the art school. I suppose she is thinking. She does not look like a suspicious subversive. Just as I am deciding to creep away again she says, out of the blue, "Fancy some chocolate?"

I freeze. It feels as if she is talking to me, then I wonder if she has one of those hands-free devices people sometimes talk into as they walk around. I stand absolutely still, as if I am playing statues at the camp, and wait.

The journalist is still looking straight ahead. Then she speaks again. "You'll get wet feet standing in the marshes like that. Much better to sit on this bench and have some chocolate." She adds, as an afterthought, "It's very good. Belgian. My kids love it."

Now I know she is talking to me. I am amazed she even realises I am here. If I did not know that she was okay, a contact of Skye's, I would be really scared, and perhaps I would run away. I do like chocolate, though.

I squelch out of the boggy land where the reeds are and approach the bench. The journalist is not at all what I expected. I see now that she does not have a hood up at all, she is wearing one of those head coverings you sometimes see in newspapers, and her skin is quite tanned, like Firefly's.

I sit on the bench next to her. "How did you know I was there?" I ask.

She takes a bar of chocolate out of her bag. It is quite large, but she snaps it in half and gives me a whole portion. She just breaks off one square for herself and pops it into her mouth before answering.

"I've got boys of my own," she says.

"In Sweden?" I ask. "How many?"

"Three," she says. "Do you like the chocolate?"

The chocolate is not as sweet as our chocolate, and it has ginger in it, and something else I cannot identify. It is very good indeed.

"I do," I tell her. "How old are they?"

"Eleven, seven and three," she says. "None of them is as good at sneaking up on people as you."

I think about that. "Do people in Sweden need to be good at sneaking up on people?" I ask.

She laughs. "No, not at all!" she says. "It is just a game!" Then she asks, "Do you need to be good at sneaking up on people?"

I stall, using the last of my half of the chocolate as a reason not to answer at once. It could be a trick question. Still, the truth is we do not really have to be good at sneaking up at all, we have to be good at hiding, or at looking like different sorts of people than we really are, so I say, "No, it's just a game too."

I decide that she is quite a pretty lady. She is not young but she has a kind face, and she seems content just to sit there, not asking me loads of questions. She eats another square of chocolate then gives the rest to me. "I'm just at that age," she says, "where a middle-aged woman starts to put on weight."

I say, "Do you miss your boys when you're away?" I am thinking of Skye. I asked her once whether she missed me on her travels and she said, "All the time."

"I don't go away that often," says the journalist. "Amar, that's my husband, is editor of a magazine in Sweden, where we live. I write a column each month, working mostly from home." She smiles sideways at me. "He earns enough for all of us, really."

"You're a long way away now," I point out. "Your boys will miss you. And Amar."

"This is an exception," she says. She has quite a strong accent but her English is easy to understand. "Something I'm doing partly for myself."

I nearly ask her why she is interested in homeless people and the feckless, but just in time I remember that she does not know I have any connection with Skye, and probably it would be best to keep it like that. So instead I say, "What are you doing? Why is it for yourself?"

She takes a deep breath and says, "You are a very inquisitive boy!" She chuckles. "In Sweden they tell us that your education, here in England, is designed nowadays to stop you asking too many questions. It doesn't seem to be very effective!"

"Oh," I say, "I'm not typical."

The woman is quiet again. It is beginning to get a bit murky, the way it does at this time of the year when the evenings are closing in.

"Do you have a name?" asks the woman. I am surprised. Even Baby Girl had a name, although of course it was only temporary.

"Everyone in England has a name!" I tell her. "Don't they in Sweden?"

She laughs quite loudly. "Yes!" she says. "Yes, they do!" Then she stops laughing. "I meant, are you willing to tell me your name?"

Of course, I am not. I think quickly, and remember Vishna calling me *Edward* when the attendance officers were suspicious of us. I say, "Edward Pearson."

"Nice to meet you, Edward Pearson," says the woman, holding out her hand to shake mine. "I'm Liliane Saker."

"You are the first Swedish person I have met," I say. "What is the thing you are doing, just for yourself?"

The woman says, "Well..." as if she is deciding what to tell me, or how to explain. Then she says, "Amar and I are first-generation Swedes. We always looked up to the UK – the country that used to include England – and if the chance had been there we might have settled here, rather than Sweden. Then everything here changed, and we hear such terrible things... I think, it could have been us. Deported. Or in labour camps. It could have been my boys."

I say, "They wouldn't put your boys in labour camps. They'd put them in care."

The woman continues as if I had not interrupted. "There are so few opportunities for reporters to visit this country now, then the PON, that's – oh, that's just a sort of journalist governing body – they had an invitation to send a reporter here to see for ourselves how much press freedom there is in England. Because Swedish papers were saying there is not much. So I applied, and they placed me here, in Winchester, at the university School of Journalism."

I think about that. I say, "I always thought journalists were based in London."

The woman smiled sadly. "You always thought correctly!" she says. "They've put us all in backwaters. I'm here, one of my colleagues is in a town called Hereford, and another is in Hull. We can't really see anything that is going on." She frowns, then seems to cheer up. "Still," she says, "I like my students, and I'm doing a bit of independent researching of my own, which turns out to be fascinating. And it's only for one semester."

She looks at me again. It is really getting dark now. She says, "I don't suppose you know much about homeless people, do you, Edward Pearson?"

I jump up, off the bench. I say, "It is nearly dark! I should be home for my tea. My mum will kill me," and I run down the track towards the exit.

I hear her calling, "Edward!" but I do not look back. I am just a bit afraid that she has guessed what I am.

"Edward!" I hear her calling again as I round the corner. "I'll be here, on this bench, most days at this time…"

I do not respond. I do not pause. The volunteer man has gone from the entrance. I slow to a casual walk and stroll along the road towards the pizza place that flooded in the storm. My heart is beating hard. When the road narrows I look behind me. She is not following me.

When I get back to the shelters Skye says, "Oh, there you are!" Then she says, "Oh, Giorgio, look at your shoes!"

I say, "Sorry, Skye," and feel relieved that she does not ask me any more questions.

★ ★ ★

Vishna is not sure if she wants to go north with everyone else. Well, not *with* everyone, because of course they will go

117

in small groups, by different routes, with different people helping them. She says to me, as we sit by the Professor's fire while the Professor sleeps, "You know, Giorgi, I've never been this free before. I'm sort of sad to give it up so soon."

"They say you're free in Scotland," I point out. "Isn't that why they're all going?"

"Mm." I can tell Vishna is not convinced. Then she says, "Skye thinks I could go to art school there, perhaps in Glasgow. Pick up where I left off."

She does not sound too keen. "Wouldn't that be good?" I ask. "You might become a famous artist one day."

Vishna rubs her eyes and flicks her hair away from them. It is getting quite long and straggly, but it looks good if she plaits it, and it shines with almost blue lights in it when it is newly washed. She says, "I'm not quite sure…"

The Professor gives a snort in her sleep. She is sitting up straight but her head keeps falling forward and her mouth is open.

Vishna says, "It doesn't seem quite right – escaping so soon, and then having a normal life. I feel I ought to be doing something for my country, not running away from it."

I think about that. It sounds good, but "What could you do?" I ask.

"That's the problem," says Vishna, slowly.

★ ★ ★

The Old Man wants to have a serious talk with me. Skye passes on the message, and I walk up the Hill into the trees and find him piling up wood in a low, thatched shelter by the fire. It is his wood store, and he is stocking up, ready for the winter.

"Help me with these, will you, Giorgio?" he says. Someone, probably Sputnik or Spanner-in-the-Works, I think, has been chopping up wood into useable sizes and it just needs to be piled up under the thatch. It is a very organised woodpile, with the small bits for kindling on one side and really large pieces at the other side. It looks like a lot, but I know from experience that you can get through a great deal of wood in one fire circle in a very short time, once the winter sets in. It has been a problem, getting enough wood, for a couple of years, and the men and bigger kids have had to go a long way to stock up. Nobody other than the Old Man has been stocking up this winter, of course.

I say, "Who will help you glean enough wood when this is all gone?" Then I say, "I will!"

"Thank you," says the Old Man. "And we must think about the Professor too."

I realise that if I am here on the Hill, alone with two old people, I could have quite a lot of responsibility. I find myself hoping that Vishna does stay, so that she can help.

We sit by the fire and drink bitter tea. The Old Man dribbles a little honey into mine when I screw up my face at the taste, and that improves it quite a lot.

"Skye tells me you really are staying behind," says the Old Man.

"I am," I agree.

"You are quite young to be on your own," points out the Old Man.

"Yes." Skye said the same thing, but I have made up my mind.

"You are staying so that you can search for your parents," says the Old Man. He hands me a biscuit. It is the sort that Little Bear's mum makes.

"Yes."

"So, what are you doing to find them?" he asks.

I swallow the last bite. I am feeling a bit guilty. "Well…" I say.

"You were going to research crosses, if I remember rightly," says the Old Man.

I feel a bit guilty. I have talked to the Music Maker and to the Professor, and I have made some notes, but that is about the limit of my research.

The Old Man sits forward on his log. He has put his mug on the ground and clasped his hands between his knees. He says, "You don't have all the time in the world, you know, Giorgio."

I wonder what he means. Does he think my parents might be in trouble somewhere, or dying? Does he know something I do not know?

He says, "Skye is letting you stay now, because we think it is safe. Relatively safe. But if something were to happen to the Professor and me... or if things were to get even tougher... If they were to decide to do a final clean up, like they did in Kent... You would just have to leave, you know. There would be no option."

I see that he is right. I see that finding my parents is not a game, like pretending to be an anti-terrorist and creeping up on the journalist.

I suppose I look worried. The Old Man smiles. He says, "I'm just saying, you need to keep going with your research. It's all a bit strange, with the others preparing to leave, but you must not be distracted. Focus on your investigations. Remember, that's why you are not going with them."

★ ★ ★

Sputnik, Scott, and his girlfriend who is not feckless, are leaving tonight. We do not know they will be going so soon until they come around to all the fires and say goodbye to everyone, and say they will see them soon, north of the border. Skye knew they were going, and how, but she did not say anything because if nobody knows, she says, nobody can accidentally let the cat out of the bag.

I say to Skye, "Now Sputnik will never find Dragon's Child and Baby Girl."

Skye says, "That train left the station weeks ago," and I think she means that all hope of that family being reunited is long gone.

I ask, "When is Little Bear's family going?" But Skye does not answer. Perhaps she does not know, or maybe she thinks it is better if I do not know. Instead she says, "You could still change your mind, Giorgi, and go with them. If you wanted to. It will be quite lonely here soon."

I say, "No, thank you. I need to find my mum and dad."

Skye sighs. "Yes," she says.

★ ★ ★

The next day I decide it is time to resume my research. I do not think there is much more I can learn from the people who are left in the camp. I say to Vishna and the Professor, "I need to go down to the city to use the library."

The Professor says, "Have you ever been in a library?"

Vishna says, "Well, it's a Saturday, so schools are out." She means that I won't arouse suspicion, the way I did when the school attendance people started looking oddly at us.

The Professor asks, "Are you back on your crosses?" Then she says to Vishna, "He won't know how to use a computer."

Vishna laughs. "Professor," she says, "they haven't called them *computers* for ages!" To me she says, "I'll come with you and show you how to use an information droid." She grins at the Professor. "I think I still have my library card!"

★ ★ ★

The library is in a wide old street with lots of restaurants, opposite a church. There are steps up to the main doors. Vishna has a plastic card in her hand with her old name on it. I have my *George Pearson* notebook and two of the pens that came in the orange box.

Vishna walks confidently towards the row of information droids. A notice says, *All users of the DeVs are required to check in at the desk.*

I whisper to Vishna, "What's a DeV?" and she says, "It's just short for *device*. Come on, let's check in."

We walk across to the desk. There is a woman in a knitted waistcoat and a man with a jumper with the flag of the Alliance on it, both wearing *Volunteer* badges, a pile of books, and several droids in charging cradles. The woman looks at us and smiles.

"Identity cards, please!" she says, cheerfully.

"Oh, bother!" says Vishna, looking at her library card. "I've picked up the wrong card!"

She places the library card on the desk, so that the friendly volunteer can see it.

"Oh, that's all right, dear," she says. "As long as you're already registered here. What about your little brother?"

I have never had an identity card, because you have to register with someone to get them, and they would put me in care. I put my *George Pearson* notebook on the desk and pretend to feel in my pockets for a card. The woman looks at the notebook.

"Oh, you go to St Mark's, do you?" she says, and beams at me. "My grandson went there. He loved it. They've moved to Oxford now." She sighed. "I miss them," she says.

"I've lost my identity card," I say. I am thinking, *They will turf us out now.*

But instead the woman says, "Well, we don't really need your ID if you go to St Mark's. They will have done all the checks. And your sister here is already a member of the library." She smiles at us both again. "So, how can I help you?"

Vishna says, "My brother's doing a project about symbols and logos. We want to look up crosses on an information droid. May we do that?"

"Of course you can, dear!" says the woman, and passes Vishna a card. "You'll know how it works."

"Of course," says Vishna, and smiles at the woman. "Come on," she says to me. "You'll have all your homework done by lunchtime at this rate!"

As we settle at the table and slot in the card to wake up the android, we hear the volunteer man say, "You should really have insisted on seeing their IDs, you know."

"Don't be ridiculous," says the woman, sounding a bit disgruntled. "You can see at a glance that they come from a respectable family!"

★ ★ ★

We have two hours free on the android, which is more than enough. We look up *cross symbol* first, and there is a mass of information but no mention of crosses in the letter Q. Then Vishna suggests we do a search stating *Cross in Q,* and we find lots of pictures of different crosses, but none at all with the letter Q around the cross.

"Perhaps it was a secret society," whispers Vishna.

"Maybe it doesn't mean anything at all," I whisper back. I am very disappointed. I thought information droids could tell you absolutely anything.

"Perhaps it has been blocked," suggested Vishna. Then she says, "We ought to print something out, to look convincing."

We find a page with the title *Christianity and the New Alliance.* It is all about the Christian values demonstrated by our two countries, the United States and England, and there are lots of different crosses to illustrate it.

"Perfect!" says Vishna and asks very politely, "May we print this out?"

The woman is having her break so it is the man we have to speak to. He says, "Up to five pages for free, then 50 cents a page."

We print out the first two pages, say "Thank you" to the man, and leave.

When we get outside Vishna looks around to see if anyone is watching us. Then she screws up the pieces of paper and puts them in the litter bin by the bus stop.

"Such rubbish!" she says, muttering more to herself than to me. "The Alliance doesn't demonstrate any Christian values at all!"

Then she cheers up. "Oh well," she says, "while we're in the city we might as well have a milkshake!"

★ ★ ★

The camp looks really strange when we arrive home. The large bikers' shelter has been taken down and the wooden poles have been removed. All that is left to show that it was ever there is a small pile of black bin-bag plastic, weighed down with a piece of wood, and worn patches in the grass. Firefly's shelter has gone, and Limpy's has had all the thatch removed. Big Bear and Little Bear are helping to carry all the wood from dismantled huts up to the trees. I expect they will add it to the Old Man's winter fuel supply. The earthworks look bigger without the shelters standing close to them, and not as friendly, and our fire circle seems to be out in the middle of nowhere now that Sputnik's shelter has gone.

The Professor is standing by her fire, leaning on her two mismatched sticks, looking a bit confused. I cannot see Skye anywhere.

We go over to the Professor, and Vishna says, "Lunchtime, Professor!"

The Professor's brow clears and she smiles at us. "Hello, you two," she says, sitting down creakily on her high log. "We are experiencing a time of change!"

"We are," I agree.

Vishna says, "We brought back fresh apples and one-day-old pastries for lunch." She finds the Professor's tin plate and puts some of the food on it, but Vishna and I eat from our hands, brushing the crumbs onto the ground.

We have just about finished, and Vishna is telling the Professor about the failure of our mission in the library, when Skye arrives.

"Any luck?" she asks us, but does not wait for an answer. She sits on my log, next to me, and says to the three of us, "It's decision time!"

"Is it?" asks the Professor, and I realise that she is becoming a bit muddled with all the changes that are happening.

Vishna moves across to the Professor and puts a hand on her arm, to stop her from feeling too worried. "What do we have to decide?" she asks Skye.

Skye takes a deep breath. "Well, first of all," she says, "I need to know who is staying and who is going. Giorgi, this is your last chance if you want to go with Little Bear."

The Professor says, rather grumpily, "I'm not going anywhere."

I am a bit disheartened by our failure to find out anything about my cross and Q symbol, but I do not feel at all like giving up, so I say, "I'm staying too."

Vishna looks from the Professor to me, and back again. Then she says, "Well, that settles it. I'm also staying!"

Skye takes a deep breath. I think she is pleased to hear that Vishna will be around, to look after me.

"Right," she says. "So be it!"

I am waiting for Skye to say something more. I know her. There is a sort of look about her, as if she is thinking about the way to tell us something. Then she leans forward and looks at the Professor. She says, "We don't think it's a good plan for your shelter to stay here, out in the open." She looks at Vishna. "Nor yours," she adds. She looks away from the fire, towards the earthworks. She says, "We want to give the impression that everyone has left. We want them to think the last group of homeless has gone, that they've won. The way they seem to have won in Kent."

"Ye-es," says Vishna thoughtfully. "That's a good plan."

The Professor says, "But Skye, I really cannot go anywhere. I can't *walk* anymore. You know that!"

Skye puts her hand on the Professor's other arm, the one Vishna is not already holding. "I know, I know," she says, comfortingly. "We are only thinking of moving you a few feet, out of sight of the city, closer to the Old Man."

The Professor is still looking upset. Vishna says, looking at the Professor and talking to her almost as if she is a kid – a younger kid than me – "That's a really good idea. And will Giorgi and I live close to the Old Man too?"

Skye looks gratefully at Vishna. "Absolutely," she says. "That's the plan."

The Professor is still looking worried. "I don't know…" she says.

Vishna pats her arm. She says, "Leave it to us, Professor. You have your afternoon nap, and Giorgi and I will move your shelter. You'll love it! Just wait and see!"

★ ★ ★

I have never seen where the Old Man has his hut. I follow Skye, carrying some of the stones that mark out our fireplace. We go into the woods, past the Old Man's fire circle, to where the Hill begins to slope down on the other side. It feels quite different here. There are far more bushes, and in the background, all the time, you can hear the whine of traffic on the bypass. I do not see the Old Man's shelter until we are almost on top of it. There are thorn bushes all around with the last few, mouldy looking blackberries still hanging onto the branches. There is a smaller fire circle here too, the sort one person might build just for himself, and another woodpile. The Old Man is nowhere to be seen.

Skye says, "We thought your shelters could be just here…" She walks a few steps to a place where smaller saplings and brambles seem to be fighting it out for space, and I see that there is another small clearing. She says, "There is certainly room for two shelters here."

Vishna is looking thoughtful. She says to me, "Giorgi, could you bear to share with me? If we make two rooms?"

"Oh, yes!" I say. "Then the Professor can have her own shelter."

Skye wades through long grass into the clearing. "The Hill slopes this way," she says. "And that way is west. The worst of the weather comes from the west, so if it were me, I'd put the shelters here… and here. With the entrances here…"

Vishna says, "And the Professor's shelter should be this one," she goes to stand in the place she means, "so that she can see our shelter easily, and the way to the Old Man's."

Skye says, "You won't bother the Old Man, will you? He's used to being on his own." She is looking a bit worried.

Vishna says, "No, don't worry, Skye. It'll be good."

By the time the Professor wakes up we have moved her shelter and I am carrying the last of her belongings away to her new home. Walking Tall and Big Bear make a sort of chair with their hands and carry her carefully through the copse and over to the new shelter, and sit her gently on her familiar tall log. She looks confused again, but not unhappy, and Vishna says to me, "Will you stay with her, while we move our shelter?"

By the time dusk comes both shelters are up. Skye and Vishna have used the old canvas from Skye's tent to build our hut. It is larger than the original one, and the red curtain does not fully divide the two rooms, but it feels warm and familiar to me.

I say to Skye, "Now you don't have a shelter."

And she says, "No, not anymore," and I think it is very sad. "But I dare say you'll let me doss here, when I visit?"

So I say, "Of course we will!" and I feel a bit better.

Vishna says, "I'm making dinner now; are you staying, Skye?" but Skye says not, gives me a hug and heads off towards the top of the Hill again.

The next day, when Vishna has made breakfast for the Professor and for us, and the fireplace is tidy and clean, so as not to attract vermin, Vishna and I walk back through the trees to our old camp. Everything has gone. The shelters have all been taken down. The stones from the fire circles have gone. There are worn patches here and there, and a hollow where Little Bear and Dylan wanted to create a paddling pool, but that is all. The people have all gone.

I say to Vishna, "I didn't say goodbye to anyone. Not even Skye!"

"Probably best that way," says Vishna.

★ ★ ★

I don't know if the grown-ups decided it among themselves when I was not around, or how it came about, but there seems to be an agreement that none of us will go over to the Old Man's shelter. The Professor becomes much brighter over the next couple of days. I think she is becoming accustomed to the changes, and I can tell that she likes to have Vishna around. On the second morning after everyone left, while we are crouching in our shelters eating breakfast, watching a steady drizzle drift across the hillside, the Professor says, "We need to tell the People that everyone has gone."

"Yes," says Vishna, looking surprised. "I hadn't thought of that." Then she adds, "I never knew how it worked with them. How do we make contact?"

"I know," I say, "Sort of. I know where to meet them, but I don't know which nights they come."

Vishna says, "We'll just have to go to the meeting place every night until we see them."

Vishna and I spend our first few days working out the details of our new life. A lot of the people who left have given us bits and pieces of food, but we will need to sort out our own systems for gleaning. The fruit and vegetable man at the market will help, of course, and Vishna thinks the art school cafeteria throws out quite a lot of food. We think we might have to fill our water bottles from the river, which seems a bit risky, but there is still half a crate left of the good stuff the People gave us, so in the meantime we agree that wherever we go we will keep our eyes open for outside taps.

Each night we go down to the lay-by where the People Who Must Be Saints gave us the chocolate bars that time when I was allowed to help. We wait in the shadows, but nobody comes, and we give up, three nights in a row, when the cathedral clock strikes one. On the fourth night Vishna says, "I think they must have heard that everyone has gone."

As she says it, we hear the whine of the electric van. Its lights are off, and it is going very slowly. It pulls up more or less where it did last time, and we all wait, just as we did before. Then the driver's door slides open and someone climbs out.

It is not one of the People who was there last time. This person is smaller, dressed in dark clothes with a hood up. We walk out into the moonlight. The van driver does not go to the back of his vehicle, and he seems to have nobody with him.

"Hi!" whispers Vishna.

"Hi!" whispers the van driver. He walks a bit closer to us, and I see that it is a girl. Not a nearly grown-up girl like Vishna, but a young girl, maybe a year or two older than me.

"Do you live on the Hill?" she murmurs, and her voice sounds hoarse, deeper than you would expect from a girl.

Vishna whispers back, "Nobody lives in that camp now. They've all gone. We came to tell you."

The girl is quiet for a moment. Then she says, "Did they arrest them? They have arrested all our adults – everyone who was at Meeting on Sunday."

"Wow!" says Vishna. "*All* of them?"

"Everyone who was at Meeting," the girl says, "and the little ones who were in the crèche."

Vishna says, "What will you do?"

We cannot see the girl's face. She stands very still for a moment, then she says, "Anyhow, I just came to tell you that we cannot help anymore."

Nobody moves. Then Vishna says, "If *you* ever need help, come around the back of the Hill."

The girl does not answer. She just stands there a moment longer, then goes back to her van.

After she has driven away, Vishna says to me, "She'll survive."

"How do you know?"

"Because she didn't let anything slip," says Vishna. "I asked her how she would survive, but she didn't answer. We don't know anything at all about her. If we were being questioned, there would be nothing we could give away."

"But if they question her," I point out, as we start to climb the Hill again, "she will know where to find us."

Vishna reaches out to hold my hand. She says, "That was a

risk we had to take. They've helped us all this time, the People. We have to be ready to help them."

"Yes," I say. "That's right."

★ ★ ★

New customs begin to develop. We find a tap in a garden belonging to an old cottage near the river. There is always a hosepipe rolled up on a stand next to it. I say, "This is so that the woman can water her garden."

Vishna says, "This is so that the woman's *gardener* can water the garden!"

We are on our way home from the art school, carrying all sorts of strange food. Earlier Vishna collected bruised bananas and cabbages which the caterpillars had been at, from the fruit and vegetable man. I stay at the camp with the Professor, who has decided to teach me some French and to keep me on the ball with my maths and English. I cannot go into the city on weekdays because of police and school attendance officers.

We go to the big fire circle in the copse if we want to talk to the Old Man. We call, "Old Man! Old Man!" just as we did when there was a whole camp looking out over the earthworks at the city. Then the Old Man comes and makes tea, and we talk about things. Vishna gives him one quarter of everything we glean, and he gives us herbs for tea, and some smelly stuff to smear on the Professor's leg, where an ulcer has appeared. He always asks after the Professor but I do not think they ever meet.

One day, Vishna and I are sitting there, drinking mint tea, when the Old Man says, "So, how's your research going, Giorgio?"

I am surprised. Ever since the rest of the camp disbanded it seems as if Vishna and I have spent all our time just working out how to survive.

"I haven't done anything since the others left," I admit.

The Old Man is quiet. Vishna, sitting next to me, is very still. At last the Old Man says, "If you don't try hard to find them now, you might regret it when you grow up."

Then he says, "But of course, it is a long time since you were separated from them. If you want to give up, that's perfectly reasonable."

"I don't want to give up…" I say. "It's just…"

The Old Man sits forward, looking serious. He says, "Giorgio, you don't need to explain to me. As long as you are happy in your own mind about what you are doing…"

I say, "I'll work out a plan."

The Old Man sits back on his log. He says, "Well, it's good to see you both, as always." And we know it is time to leave.

★ ★ ★

It is cold at night now. There was frost on the ground and on the scraggly blackberry thorns when we woke up this morning. It is Vishna's first winter in a shelter, and I tell her about going for a jog just before bed to get warm, and about sleeping with all your clothes on. We are concerned about the Professor. She starts to cough, and Vishna says she will go into the city to find something warmer for the Professor to wear at night. The Professor tells us not to fuss, but we are both worried.

The Professor is still teaching me. She says I have an appalling French accent but that my English is fine and that I'm never going to have problems with maths. I have made a plan for continuing my research but it means I need to go down into the city, and it is really only safe to do that at the weekends.

Then Vishna comes back with a huge bundle wrapped up in a bin bag. She unrolls it in front of our fire for the Professor to see.

The Professor says, "I can't wear that!" and looks horrified. It is a rather worn-out-looking fur coat.

Vishna laughs, "No, you can't!" she agrees. "We could fit two of you into this!" Then she says, "But it will make a brilliant blanket to keep you warm at night."

The Professor says, "But it's an animal fur! I've never been near an animal fur in all my seventy-five years!"

Vishna does not look at all taken aback. "Me neither," she says. "It's wrong to kill animals for fashion. Everyone knows that! But you know, Professor, Native Americans used to use animal furs. The Blackfoot, in Canada. It was not for fashion. It was not abusing nature. It was using the abundance of the land."

"Mm," says the Professor. She leans forward, resting one hand on her stick to balance, and strokes the fur. "I suppose we did not kill it," she says. "It would be dead, whether I used it as a blanket or not."

I ask, "Where does it come from, Vishna?"

Vishna looks slightly ashamed. "Well," she says, "there was a pile of stuff outside the charity shop. The shop doesn't open until ten on Fridays. It was in the pile."

The Professor says, "So somebody wanted to give it away?"

"Yes," agrees Vishna.

The Professor strokes the fur again. "Thank you, Vishna," she says.

Then Vishna says to me, "And next week is half term. All the schools are out. You can go into the city and do your research."

★ ★ ★

My plan is to visit as many churches as I can, starting in the middle of the city and working out. There are two buildings that really interest me, and I have noticed that neither is

133

locked up. People come and go to them all day. One church is under an arch near a big stone monument called *the Butter Cross*. When I was little and Skye sometimes brought me into the city, there were often beggars close to this church, or demonstrators around the Butter Cross, but you never see those people now. I expect the beggars are all in labour camps. And the demonstrators? In prison, I suppose, like the People Who Must Be Saints.

It is Monday morning and I am awake early. It is still dark and my nose is cold, although the rest of me is snug in my sleeping bag, with a pile of blankets wrapped around me. I can hear the Professor snoring loudly in her shelter, and Vishna is tossing and turning a bit, getting ready to wake up. I creep out of the shelter and examine the fire. We put a thick log on it the night before, and it is still smouldering, but only just. It is hard to keep a fire in all night. I take a handful of kindling from our thatched woodpile and prop it up against the log, then blow gently. Once it has caught alight I add larger pieces of wood. By the time Vishna crawls out of the shelter, yawning and stretching, with her plaits looking frayed after being slept on all night, the water for tea is boiling.

"You're up early," she says, lacing up her trainers. "Oh, look!"

There is a small tin on one of the hearth stones. The Old Man does that sometimes. He brings little gifts while we are asleep or away from the shelter. This time it is blackberry tea, which is good for the Professor's cough but also delicious with breakfast. Vishna spoons some into a second can and adds hot water. We leave it next to the fire to keep warm.

"Any plans for today?" asks Vishna. She is rooting around in an old biscuit tin where we keep food, and bringing out cereal bars which, I suspect, might have been stolen.

"It's half term," I remind her. "I'm going into Winchester to look at churches. I'm going to try to find my symbol."

"I'll walk down with you," says Vishna, and pours blackberry tea into three mugs. "I want to look behind the art college union building, and talk to Fruit Man." She unwraps two cereal bars and puts them on a plate, then she crouches at the entrance to the Professor's shelter. "Knock, knock!" she says. "Professor, it's morning. I've brought you some breakfast."

★ ★ ★

Down in the city everything looks a bit drab. It is one of those cold, grey days when people keep the lights in their houses on all day long, and everyone who owns a coat (unlike me) seems to be huddled down into it. Only the teenagers look carefree. There is a group standing by the Guildhall. They are wearing camouflage jackets with the old Confederate flag on cloth badges on the shoulders, although you can tell they are English by their accents. You see that symbol everywhere nowadays. They are not really doing anything, just hanging around and talking loudly. They give Vishna a sort of look as we walk past, and one of them whistles, but they ignore me.

Vishna heads off towards the art school and I walk on up the High Street, looking at the Halloween displays in the shop windows and feeling good. Nobody even glances at me. They are all hurrying this way and that, trying to get out of the cold. A small child, holding the hand of a grown-up, drops a mitten, and I pick it up and run after them. "Excuse me," I say, and hand it back.

"Thank you," says the woman. She looks too old to be the child's mother. A grandparent, I suppose, caring for her grandchild while the mother is at work.

The church under the arch is already unlocked, and the lights are on inside. It looks very welcoming. I know a lot of tourists like to go to this church, and there is a box at the entrance asking for donations to help with the upkeep. I am tempted to try and take the money out. We could really use some cash. But the thought that I am in a church makes me pause, and then I realise that anyone walking past might see me. Instead I just go in, and sit on a chair, and look around.

I know now that the table at the front is called an *altar*; the Professor has been teaching me these things, although I am not sure of the point of altars. They are to do with sacrifices, I think, but Christians do not make sacrifices. I think perhaps they did in the old days, when Christianity was just taking over from other religions. There is a cross on the altar, but there is no image of Jesus on the cross, which should mean the church is Protestant. I think, *I'm learning*! Then I feel a little bit sad, because it was not that long ago that I heard Skye say, *They're learning something new every day.* It seems like such a long time since I saw Skye.

There are other crosses around, if you look carefully. The books at the back, with poems in them, have crosses on the covers. The big bible on a stand has a cross on the cover, and the cloth bookmark has a cross on it too. None of the crosses have a Jesus on them, and none of them have a Q.

Some visitors come in and look around. One of the men has picked up a leaflet about the history and is reading it rather loudly to the rest of the group. I sit quietly and wait for them to go. Then one of the women pats me on the shoulder and says, in a strong American accent, "Sorry to have disturbed your meditations, young man." Then off they go.

Of course, I have not been meditating. I have been listening to their words, and thinking about the deep red colour of *medieval*, which is a word they use a lot, and waiting to have the church to myself. Outside, people are bustling around, coming and going past the glass doors, but nobody is paying any attention to me. I stand up and go to the side of the room, where there is a rather muddled pile of old-looking books.

This church is very clean and neat, a comfortable sort of place, and it is odd that this ramshackle heap of books should be piled here. I look through them, but there is nothing of interest to me.

The next church on my list is quite different. It is a pop-up church. It appeared last summer, where a clothes shop used to be. In the windows, where there used to be male figures without heads one side of the door, and female figures without heads on the other, all wearing trendy clothes, there are now posters and books. The posters say encouraging things, like *The Lord knows what you need before you ask Him*, or *Come to me, all you who are weary and burdened, and I will give you rest*. There are pictures of smiling children and teenagers on these posters, and family groups where everyone has very white teeth. Most of the posters don't have crosses on them, but a few do. I stand and look in the window at all the pictures of happy people and think they look like advertisements for health insurance.

A man comes out, smiling and looking pleased to see me, as if he and I are friends.

"Good morning, young man," he says. "Can I be of any help to you on this fine day?"

I look up and down the High Street. It does not look as if anybody else thinks it is a fine day. Still, I like his cheerfulness. I say to him, "I'm interested in finding out more about the cross."

The man looks really, seriously, taken aback. "My goodness!" he says. Then, "Well!" He looks as if someone has taken his breath away, the way Limpy looked after Big Bear pushed him over the earthworks. He gulps, then he says, "Perhaps you would like to come in?"

Inside it is set out like a sort of café, with small round tables and easy chairs, all facing towards the rear of the shop. There, on the back wall, there is a cross, large and flat with no Jesus on it, but with flashing lights draped round it. Below the cross is a table which, I think, could be an altar or it could just be a useful piece of furniture.

The man says, "Would you like something to drink?" and he brings out a bottle of fizzy drink from a cupboard to one side. I know about that stuff; Skye told me. She said it is bad for you, that it rots the teeth and makes you hungry for sugary food. I say, "Please may I just have water?"

The man puts the bottle away, but he does not give me any water. I realise that he is not quite sure what to say to me.

I think I will help him. I say, "I'm doing a project for school, about symbols. I have found that the cross is a very important symbol, with lots of different meanings."

"Oh no!" says the man. "It only has one meaning. It means salvation. It means eternal life. It means never having to worry about your sins, or about hell, or about the future. It means joy and peace and knowing right from wrong."

I say, "That sounds like quite a lot of meanings." Then I think some more, and I say, "But I never worry about my sins, or hell, or the future." The last part is not quite true because I do worry a little, when I wake up in the night sometimes, about being put into care, but of course I do not tell the man that.

The man has gone quite red. "Well, you should worry about those things!" he says.

Now I am muddled. He has just told me that the cross is a symbol to tell me I do not need to worry! I wonder if the man is quite clear in his head about the meaning of the cross. Anyhow, I need some clarification. I say to the man, "What is hell?"

Until that moment I had just thought it was a rude sort of word. People say, "Go to hell!" if they do not like you, but I have never considered that it might be a place where I might actually go.

"Oh, dear!" says the man. There is sweat on his forehead

now, and he tugs at his shirt collar. I am not trying to be difficult, but obviously the man is finding my questions hard to answer. "Hell is the place where all sinners go, when they leave this mortal life," he says.

"But..." Did not the man say, a few minutes ago, that because of the cross we did not need to worry about hell?

The man gulps. He says, "You have to be born again. You have to give your life to Christ. You have to lay all your sins at the foot of the cross, and you will have eternal life." A sort of relief shows on the man's face. He has obviously said what he wanted to say, although, in fact, it has made no sense at all to me. I vaguely wonder whether the table underneath the flashing cross is the place to lay your sins, but that does not make sense either. I do not think sins are things that you can put down and pick up.

I do not feel as if I am getting anywhere. The man has sat back in his chair, as if he is waiting for me to answer. I wonder what he wants me to say.

Then I see that the man is wearing a small badge on the lapel of his slightly shiny suit jacket. It has a shape like a fish, with a cross inside it.

I say, "What does your badge mean?"

The man looks down at his lapel, and it makes him have not a double chin, but a triple one. He smiles, as if I have asked a good and easy question. He says, "The fish means *Jesus Christ, God's Son, Saviour*, and the cross means I am saved."

I vaguely wonder what he has been saved from. Did he grow up in care? Did somebody put him in a labour camp? But the interesting thing is that there is a cross, a plain cross like the one on my symbol, inside another symbol. I ask him, "Is the fish a secret symbol?"

"It was once," says the man, "when Christians were persecuted. But not now, of course."

Now, I think, we are getting somewhere. This man seems

to know the sorts of things I am trying to research, even if his explanations are rather confusing. I say, "And what would a cross inside a letter Q mean?"

The man's face goes rather blank. "Oh," he says, "there is no such symbol as that."

It seems the man cannot help me any further. I stand up. "Thank you for answering my questions," I say. "I will write it all in my project."

I start to walk towards the door. "Wait a minute!" the man says. He reaches to the shelf where the fizzy drinks are kept and brings out a little booklet, the size of a library card, with cartoon characters on it. He says. "Why don't you read this? The best thing a young person can do is to give his heart to Jesus!"

The booklet is called *Now or Never*. I say, "Thank you," and leave the shop. As I go I hear the man say to himself, "Praise the Lord! A real lost sheep!"

★ ★ ★

Vishna has apples and a cabbage in her bag, along with two very dented tins containing baked beans. I meet her, quite by accident, in the High Street, and we walk back the long way, round the Hill and past the public footpath, to our secret track. We are being careful to leave and arrive by different routes, so that we do not leave evidence of too much coming and going. Our shelters are well hidden, even from this angle. The only clue that there are people living there is a thin wisp of smoke from our fire, and on a grey day like this I do not think anyone would notice it, unless that person was really looking for signs of life, and perhaps not even then.

The path we are using winds in and out of the brambles. We have to look where we are going, because the thorns hook on to our clothes, and it is slippery underfoot. That must be the reason that we do not see the Professor until we are right into our tiny clearing.

She is lying on the ground, looking crooked and very still. Her tall log has fallen over, and there is a mug half filled with blackberry tea standing on a stone.

We both rush towards her. "Professor!" calls Vishna, and bends down to look at her face. Then she stands up again, very slowly. "She's dead!" she says to me. "The Professor's dead."

I kneel down beside the old lady. I do not believe Vishna. I shake the Professor's shoulder, and I say gently, "Wake up, Professor! Wake up!"

Her head rolls a little, sideways. Her eyes are open and there is a little smile on her face. For a second I think she is playing a trick on us, but she is not blinking. Vishna reaches down and brushes her eyes closed.

"Why did you do that?" I say, and I am angry. I shake the Professor's shoulder again. "Wake up! Wake up!" I cry.

She does not move. She cannot wake up. She is dead.

I stand up and look at Vishna. Vishna is crying, big tears rolling down her face. She sobs, "We shouldn't have left her alone! She died all alone out here, and nobody was with her! Oh, Giorgi!"

I am crying too. We just stand there next to each other, and neither of us knows what to do.

Finally, Vishna says, "Let's put her back in her shelter, then we ought to go and find the Old Man."

★ ★ ★

The Old Man is tending his herbs, although nothing much grows at this time of the year. We rush towards him, saying, "Old Man! Old Man!"

He stands up and looks at us, very calmly. He says, "How nice to see you." It makes me feel silly for crashing into the Old Man's turf like this. I say, "Old Man, the Professor is dead!"

His face still looks calm. He takes a deep breath. Vishna is standing beside me now, the tears still pouring down her cheeks. He says to Vishna, "Is this true?"

Vishna nods. She says between sobs, "We just came back from the city. She was lying on the ground, by the fire. She's dead."

The Old Man brushes the earth off his hands and says, "Let me see."

We all walk back through the copse and Vishna points to the Professor's shelter. "We put her back in there," she says.

The Old Man bends down and looks in. Then he kneels, the way he does when he is tending his herbs, and looks at the Professor more closely. He mutters something to himself, and then he comes out backwards and slowly stands up again. He is smiling.

"She died happy," he says.

Neither of us answers. He says, "She died with a smile on her face."

I know this to be true. I do not feel quite so bad about her being all alone. I wonder what she was smiling about.

Vishna says, "Old Man, what are we going to do?" She is crying much more than me, and I think how much she loved the Professor, and how much the Professor must have loved her.

The Old Man says, "We are going to go and have a snack and a hot drink. Then we are going to dig a grave for the Professor." He smiles gently at the two of us. "Actually," he says, "you are going to dig the grave, because my earth-shovelling days are over!" He starts to walk towards the big fire circle in the middle of the trees. Over his shoulder he says,

"And when Skye comes back, today or tomorrow, we are going to have a funeral."

★ ★ ★

We eat the Old Man's food for our snack. He gives us hot oatmeal with bits of apple on top, and the food is comforting. It is strange to be eating with the Old Man, but rather pleasant. We drink bitter tea made less bitter with drops of honey, and Vishna stops crying and talks quite a lot to the Old Man about the Professor. The Old Man just nods and smiles, and says things like, "That is so," and "Absolutely". All the while he looks interested. After quite a long time Vishna begins to talk less quickly and more quietly. Then she stops altogether. "I'm sorry," she says to the Old Man. "She was one of the wisest people I have ever met."

The Old Man smiles. "I'm glad you knew her," he says. Then he looks at me. "I'm glad you both knew her. But now it is time we did the last loving acts we can do for her. Time to get digging!"

We make the grave just outside the large fire circle. It is hard work because underneath a thin layer of earth there is chalk, some soft and a bit green, but some white and hard. We chip away at it all afternoon, until the early autumn dusk makes it hard to see. Then the Old Man says, "We'll finish it tomorrow."

So we go back to our shelter, and Vishna makes vegetable stew with a sort of dumpling, and we eat an apple each. Then we jog up to the trees and back a couple of times to get our circulation going, and scramble into our sleeping bags while we are still warm.

"Goodnight, Professor," says Vishna as she wriggles down into her sleeping bag, on her side of the partition.

"Goodnight, Professor," I echo.

★ ★ ★

It is Skye who wakes us up. I am dreaming about Little Bear. In my dream, he is running and running, and I am trying to catch up with him. He has some cake in his hand, and I want it, but he will not share it with me.

Then a voice says, "Wake up, sleepy heads! Tea and cake for breakfast!"

And there is Skye. She is wearing a new jacket that I have not seen before, but everything else about her is so familiar and normal that it feels as if the last few weeks have not happened at all. She is smiling into the tent, just the way she did when we lived in the larger camp on the other side of the Hill.

I say, "Skye, the Professor's died."

Skye says, "Yes, I know." Then she says, "She died quickly and easily, I think. She would have wanted it like that."

We sit around the fire and eat our breakfast, and at first we just talk about the Professor, but then we start telling Skye about the other things that have happened while she has been away. I have not even told Vishna about the man in the pop-up church, and when I try to describe what happened both of them start to laugh, and they cannot stop. "That poor man!" gasps Skye, and I think it is unfair. I was polite to him all the time, and it is not my fault if he talked in circles!

★ ★ ★

We have the funeral after our snacks. We wrap the Professor up in a blanket and then in the fur coat, and Skye and Vishna lower her very gently into the grave. The Professor did not have any religious beliefs, and none of the rest of us pray either, so the Old Man says, "From the earth we came, and to the earth we return the body of our dear friend, the Professor."

Vishna adds, "May she rest in peace," and she is crying again.

Then we pile the soil and the lumps of chalk back into the hole, and the Old Man asks Vishna and me to stamp all over it. "It needs to look quite normal," explains Skye, and she scatters a few ashes from the fire on top of the grave and puts dead leaves and bits of twig around. I think that in a few days you will not be able to tell that a body has been buried there.

Vishna says, "I hate to think of the Professor out here in the cold."

Skye says, "It isn't the Professor. It's just an old body that she has left behind."

I wonder if the Professor still exists somewhere, in a new body, or perhaps as a being without a body. I do not ask, though, because how will any of them know?

Then Vishna and Skye make a meal at our hearth and bring it back to the big fire circle, where we share it with the Old Man, and Skye tells us the news, and gives us presents.

"Well," she says, "the best news first, I think?"

Vishna says, "No, let's hear the bad news first and get it over with!"

But Skye says, "There isn't really any bad news, just good, better and best."

Then she fishes a letter out of the pocket of her new jacket. She says, "The Bears are safely in Scotland. They are not going to live in Edinburgh, as I was expecting, but in a croft out on one of the islands. Last I heard, they had already applied, and it seems certain they will be accepted. It's a chance in a lifetime. Perfect for them. Giorgi, I've got a letter from Little Bear for you."

She passes it across. It is dark by now so I cannot read it, but I am happy that Little Bear is safe and was not caught and put into care.

Vishna says, "They'll love it in a croft! It won't be so different from living here!"

I think, *Tomorrow I'll find out what a croft is*. *Croft* is a comfortable word, light green with flecks of brown. It is similar to *turf*, and I think it has to do with belonging.

Skye goes on, smiling a little as she tells us more. "That's the best news. Firefly and her parents are safely across the border but they don't know where they'll go yet. The Music Maker phoned me from Aberdeen. He played a gig in a pub and they liked him, but he wants to move on, further north maybe, to live in a smaller community. That's the better news."

"So, that just leaves the good news," I say.

"The good news," says Skye, looking across the circle at me, "is that Limpy and Florence got in really easily. They asked for asylum on their way in, and when the immigration people heard how Limpy was injured they started the process at once. It will take time, but I'm sure they'll be okay."

"What about Sputnik and Scott?" asks Vishna.

"And Dylan and his dad?" I ask.

"Ah," says Skye, and glances sideways at the Old Man. "I can't say too much about them yet. But nothing has gone wrong. It's just that... well, it's just that there's no news yet."

"But there are presents!" she says. She hands two packages across the circle, a really bulky one for me and a large envelope for Vishna.

"You first," says Vishna, so I open the paper carrier bag and pull out a heavy camouflage jacket. It is similar to the ones the teenagers were wearing, although the cloth badge is on a pocket. It is lined with some sort of padding and it has a zip and Velcro at the front.

"Put it on!" demands Vishna, so I take my gilet off and pass it to Vishna, then put on my present.

It feels wonderful. The sleeves are a bit too long and the

jacket goes almost down to my knees, but it is warmer and softer than any coat I have ever worn. "Oh, thank you!" I say to Skye, and dash across the circle to give her a hug.

The Old Man is looking at Skye with raised eyebrows. Skye smiles. "No," she says, as if she is answering a question. "Bought legally with a contactless card, by a well-wisher!"

Vishna says, "Nobody will ever guess Giorgi is feckless when he's dressed like that!"

Skye smiles. "I had thought of that," she says. "But our well-wisher was more concerned about the weather."

The Old Man says, "My goodness, Giorgio, you look so grown up!"

Skye smiles, "He has changed almost beyond recognition in the last six months."

I feel embarrassed. I say, "What is your present, Vishna?"

She opens the envelope, tilting it so that the firelight shines on the documents she pulls out. There is a small, dark-coloured booklet, a little cover for it which might be leather – it is hard to tell by firelight – and a plastic envelope. For a moment Vishna looks confused.

Skye crosses the circle to sit on the log next to Vishna, on the other side from me. She takes the booklet and opens it to show Vishna whatever is printed on that page. "Your new passport," she says, "with a visa giving you the right to enter Europe and re-enter England for up to five years. You are Violet Blair, an art student at the National College of Art and Design in Dublin. If the authorities check, there really is a place for Violet, deferred while she engages in personal research."

Vishna does not say anything. She looks at Skye, then she looks across at the Old Man, then she looks back at the document in her hand.

"But…" she says.

Skye says, "You want to be in England right now, I know.

147

But five years is a long time. We think this passport will stand up to scrutiny, and it's a way of escape, if you need it. You don't have to use it."

I say, "Do I have a way of escape, Skye?"

She says, "Just tell me when you want to go, and it'll be a done deal."

Vishna is still looking at her new passport. "What about fingerprints," she says, "and iris recognition?"

"All sorted," says Skye. "Someone hacked the art school records here. Your information was all held on a database, along with some rather uncomplimentary comments about your attitude towards authority!"

I say, "What's in that envelope, Vishna?"

She looks surprised to see me sitting next to her, as if she has completely forgotten I am there. She pulls the two plastic edges of the envelope apart and takes out a small wad of bank notes. "Euros," she says. "Do they still use them?"

"Oh yes," says Skye. "For small transactions."

Vishna still looks stunned. She slowly fits the passport into its cover and puts it in the back pocket of her jeans. Then she takes it out again. "I need to keep it somewhere safe," she says.

"We'll sort that out tomorrow," promises Skye. "And now, let me tell you about the Scottish border official at the Liddersdale crossing…"

We stay up and talk until very late. The colours of our words flicker and burn around the fire circle, and we laugh a lot, and cry a little when we talk about the Professor. From the woods we cannot see the city, but Vishna and I jog once round the earthworks to get our circulation going before we go to bed, leaving Skye and the Old Man to talk about whatever it is they discuss alone. All the street lights in the city are off but we can see blue lights flashing part way up the hill opposite, that leads to the hospital.

"I hope that's not a raid," says Vishna.

"Perhaps they're just arresting burglars," I say, but I am glad we are on our Hill, not down in the city.

★ ★ ★

Skye says she can only stay for a couple of days. She moves into the Professor's hut, but I stay in our shelter with Vishna. Skye has her usual backpack, and apart from her new jacket she seems just the same as ever. Before she came back it had begun to feel as if the encampment on the other side of the Hill had been years ago, but now it feels quite recent and I find myself thinking much more about Little Bear, Dylan, Limpy and Firefly.

I read Little Bear's letter at breakfast time, sitting by the fire wearing my new jacket and feeling snug and warm despite the cold wind. It is quite a short letter, but he sounds happy. He starts by saying, We made it! and then tells me about the croft they hope to take over. I discover that a croft is like a small farm, and that they think they will mostly have sheep, but some chickens too. He tells me, Big Bear and I will go to a proper school, but Walking Tall won't have to pay any taxes until we have made some money. Then he says, We might have to choose different names but Walking Tall and the refugee people are hoping to persuade them to allow us to keep our real names. He ends his letter, Wish you were here! and for a few minutes I wish I were there too.

Then I think to myself, Giorgio, you need to find your parents! I picture me living in a croft next door to Little Bear with my mum and dad. My dad would be tall and strong, and my mum would look a bit like Vishna and would have brown hair and eyes like me, because we all come from Italy originally. Of course, I know this is just a dream, but it reminds me of why I have stayed behind.

So when Skye says, "What are you two going to do today?"

149

I say, "I want to go into the city and do some more cross research," and Vishna says, "I'll come with you."

★ ★ ★

There is a church near the top of the city, where they serve coffee in the mornings. It is the United Church, but I do not know who or what it is united with. I think I will look at the crosses there and then maybe go to the cathedral. Skye tells me you have to pay, and also says that I might want to buy a drink at the United Church, so she gives me some dollar coins.

The group of teenagers we saw before are by the Guildhall again. This time they look at Vishna first, then they notice me in my camouflage jacket and they say "Yo!" and high-five me. A traffic warden is standing there, stopping private cars from parking in the taxi places, and he smiles at the boys the way that nobody ever smiles at feckless people, but all he says is, "Now, stay on the pavement, you lot! We don't want any accidents."

When we get to the place where the street narrows, and the teenagers cannot hear us, Vishna says, "That jacket is really perfect, isn't it?" And I say, "Yes!" and feel happy and safe.

Vishna heads off for the rear of the art school cafeteria, to do some gleaning, and I walk up to the church. At first, I think there are no crosses at all on the outside of the building, then I notice that their sign is on the glass of their doors, and I feel a bit excited. It is a plain cross with no Jesus, but there is a circle around the place where the two pieces of the cross join, and the whole thing is in a shape which is almost like a rectangle, with cut-off corners. So now I have seen a cross in a fish and a cross in a rectangle. It makes me feel as if I might find a cross in a Q at any moment.

I follow other people in, to the place where they are selling hot drinks and cakes. Most of the people seem either fairly old, or younger than me. I queue up, and when I get to the table I say, "May I have some water and a bun, please?"

The woman serving says, "Wouldn't you like some squash? Or hot chocolate? It's a cold day." So I settle for hot chocolate (it is a little bit lumpy) and a bun with very pink icing on it.

There are people sitting at all the round tables. It feels quite different from the pop-up church. For one thing, there are lots of people here, and for another thing, nobody looks religious. They are just ordinary people, drinking and eating and talking quite loudly. There are a few chairs lined up against the wall, and I sit there, out of the way, and look around. Once again, I see a few crosses. Well, two, to be exact, and they are absolutely plain.

Two ladies and a man are sitting at the table nearest to me, the man facing in my direction. His coat is unbuttoned, and I can see that he has spilt food down his jumper. I think he is a bit deaf, because he talks loudly to the women and does not seem to realise that I can hear him.

"There's a lad all on his own over there," he says.

The two women turn their heads to look at me. "He's not doing any harm," says one, and turns back to their table.

"When we had children," says the elderly man, "we didn't let them wander around the town on their own."

The other woman says something I cannot hear, then the man speaks quite loudly again. "I blame the government. Women should be at home looking after their children! All this talk about fecklessness is nonsense! Why should women be obliged to work while their children are small?"

The quiet woman says something else and puts her hand on the arm of the man. The other woman says, "Best not to say things like that in public, Marcus!"

The man says, grumpily, "Don't be ridiculous! Do you think they're going to put me in a labour camp, at my age?"

The two women look around anxiously. One of them

meets my eye and smiles nervously. I grin, in a way that I hope says, "I don't mean you any harm," and then I get up and leave. As I squeeze past their table I say, "My grandpa says the same thing!" and all three of them look relieved and smile at me.

★ ★ ★

The newsagents where the post office is located has put up a screen and it shows news headlines and advertisements. Today they are forecasting a cold half-term week, and advertising careers in the military. I spend a couple of minutes looking at a film of very fit and happy young adults going over an obstacle course, then I cross the precinct by the Butter Cross, past St Lawrence's Church and across the green to the cathedral. I pay my ten English dollars and go inside.

I have been into the cathedral only once before. Skye took Dylan and me there one Sunday afternoon, when we were caught in the rain and Dylan did not have a coat. We could not wear our bin bags in the city because it showed us up as being feckless. We had only gone just inside the door because of the barriers that stop people from wandering around without paying. This time, thanks to the money Skye has given me, I have a printed ticket with a drawing of the cathedral on it, and *half price* stamped on it in red letters because I am still a kid.

I walk slowly all the way down one side of the seats, looking at all the plaques on the walls, at the notices on boards, and at the stonework itself. I do not bother to read the memorials or inscriptions, because I am really only interested in finding a Q with a cross in it. Behind the table which is an altar there are ancient-looking tiles on the floor, but you are allowed to walk on them, and some quite modern-looking paintings. There are all sorts of crosses, all over the place. Some have Jesus hanging on them and some do not. Some have two cross pieces, but most only have one. Several of them have circles around the place where the two cross pieces meet, and for a moment I think that one of these is a Q, but then I realise it is just a circle, like lots of others that I have seen.

When I have explored all down one side and up the other, I walk along the passage between the seats in the middle. Other people are just sitting on chairs looking forward. One woman seems to be kneeling down with her head in her arms. A man in a black robe is answering questions that a group of visitors are asking. Nobody pays me any attention. I start to count all the crosses I can see, but stop when I get to twenty. I wander over to the bookstall by the door, hoping to see a book or a leaflet about crosses, but I only see guidebooks and postcards. The woman asks me if she can help me, but I just say, "No, thank you," and leave. I do not want to get into another conversation about sins and hell, and all those things that the man in the pop-up church tried to explain.

There are lots of ways back to the Hill from the cathedral. This time I walk past the hotel, under the car parking space and then under an arch which leads to a little back street. I have been here lots of times before and I am not really thinking about where I am going. All the houses in this street are joined together, and I wonder whether that is so with crofts on Scottish islands. It would be fun to have a bedroom next to Little Bear's, so that we could knock on the walls at night, or even talk to each other. Then I think that walls are usually made of bricks or stones, so perhaps you cannot hear through them, and I think it would be strange not to be able to hear the person on the other side of the partition breathing at night. It gives me a lonely feeling.

After a short while the buildings stop. There is a high, solid, wooden gate, and next to it a noticeboard. Someone has stuck a notice up at some time, but someone else has tried to tear it down again, so that all I can read now are the words *silence* and *peace*. Above the gate are the words *Friends' Meeting House*. The wood of the gate is broken, as if someone has tried to smash it with something heavy, and I can see through. Inside there seems to be a wild garden, very overgrown and sad-looking in the damp October weather.

There is nobody in the street. I look up and down but there are no dog-walkers, nobody pushing a buggy, nothing. I lift the latch and creep into the garden, closing the gate as quietly as I can after me.

There is a huge house to my right, with plants growing up the side of it. One of the downstairs windows has been broken at some time, and someone has put a piece of wood over it, I suppose to keep the rain out. There is graffiti on the wood, and on the white front door. *Fuck of* it says, and in my mind I change it to say *Fuck off* before I correct myself too. It is rude, and it should not say anything at all!

The building seems to be deserted. One of the windows upstairs is either open or broken, and a curtain is flapping against the outside wall. I try the door, ignoring the spray-painted instruction, but it is locked. I follow the path round the building to see more boarded-up windows at the back.

There is a large garden and a wooden hut, and a little stream runs though the garden. I wonder who the friends were, who used to meet there, and why they had a special house for meeting in. What was wrong with coffee shops and each other's homes?

Everything is overgrown. The grass is long and tangled, and a prickly branch from a rose bush stretches across the paved footpath. I think I will just walk up to the end of the garden, and then it will be snack time, and I will go back up the Hill. But as I walk under a tree on the lawn, I think I see something move to my left. I see that there is a second wooden building in among the trees, and I am sure I have seen a person duck down, out of sight, in the winter greenery.

I stand still. Nothing moves. I am beginning to think I have made a mistake, when I hear a sneeze. There is no doubt about it. Someone is there.

I half think I should just leave, right there and then. It is not my business if people are hiding, and I do not know if they are friendly or dangerous. Yet I turn and walk towards the bushes.

There are three people there, two about my age and one younger. The tallest of the three, a girl, says to me, "Go away!" Her voice is a bit gruff, as if she has a cold, and she sounds angry, or maybe frightened.

I think that they must be feckless kids, because they look damp and ragged, and maybe hungry. I forget that I am wearing my smart new camouflage jacket and that I might look quite threatening to them. I say, "Why are you hiding?"

The boy says, "We're not hiding, we're playing a game," but I feel sure he is telling a lie.

The small kid, another girl, starts to cry.

I am standing there thinking. There is something vaguely familiar about the older girl, and for a moment I cannot think what it is, then suddenly I say, "Hey! Aren't you the girl who drove the van? Are you one of the People?" I realise where I heard that hoarse voice before – at the foot of the Hill, when Vishna and I went down to explain that everyone from the camp had gone.

"What people?" says the boy. I can tell that he just wants me to go away.

I say, "Are you the people who used to bring us water and food, up on the Hill?"

The gruff girl asks, "Us?"

I explain. "There used to be a camp on the Hill. St Catherine's Hill. Homeless people. And you used to bring us food and water, in a van, a couple of times a week."

The gruff girl says, "Not us, but people from our Meeting."

I say, "We thought you might be saints."

The little girl is standing very close to the boy. She still looks terrified. I say, "I used to live in that camp."

The boy says, "You don't look like someone who lives in a homelessness place. They are scruffier than you."

"I did live there, though," I say. Then I remind the girl, "You told us that all the grown-ups who were at your Meeting were arrested."

The little girl starts to cry again. "My mummy has gone!" she wails.

"Shush!" soothes the boy. Then to me he says, "Anyhow, what's it to you?"

I say, "So how are you managing, without any adults?" I have a horrible thought. "Will they put you in care?"

"That's why we're hiding," says the hoarse girl.

The boy says, "Did you really live at that camp?"

"Yes."

"So, where do you live now?" I can tell he is still suspicious. I know it is because of my jacket. I do not look feckless at all dressed like this; I look like the little brother of a teenager who hangs around outside the Guildhall whistling at girls like Vishna, and then goes home at the end of the day to a mum and a dad who both have good jobs and can buy their children warm winter clothes.

I answer, "In a shelter," without mentioning the Hill.

"They closed all the homelessness shelters," says the tall girl. "At least a year ago."

I say, "Not that sort of shelter." Then I ask, "Where do you live?" I look at the bushes. "You can't hide there all night!"

The tall girl and the boy look at each other. "Why would he lie?" asks the girl.

The boy seems to be thinking. Then he says, "Come and see."

The wooden hut I saw first, from the path by the main

house, has windows facing towards the garden, and a French door which is closed. The boy goes to the door and opens it. We all go inside.

There is one small room in the hut. On one side, there is a row of shelves with a strange mixture of things on them: books, an open packet of flour, a few mugs and a stack of plastic beakers, and some colouring crayons, and there is a stepladder leading to a sort of inside balcony upstairs. There is very small furniture for little children, stacked under a normal sized table, and two or three armchairs. There is a beanbag, which the little girl sits on. She picks up a piece of woolly blanket and holds it to her face, and puts her thumb in her mouth.

I look around. "This is nice," I say.

"It's the children's room," says the boy. "It's where the little ones were when everyone was arrested. The grown-ups were in the large meeting room. In the House."

"Where were you?" I ask.

The girl says, "We were on a nature trail. Looking round Winchester. We were doing work on the environment."

She points to a piece of paper pinned to the wall underneath a clock. Someone has written *Protect and care for the Earth as a sacred trust,* and underneath there are some autumn leaves glued into a pattern and looking rather shrivelled up, and a picture that looks as if it has been cut out of a magazine and stuck on the paper, showing flowers in a pot.

And then I see it. Next to the unfinished display is a printed poster. It shows two children sitting with their eyes closed. There is a black boy, who looks a bit like Firefly, and a blond girl. The words say, *Take heed, dear Friends, to the promptings of love and truth in your hearts,* but the thing that makes me freeze is the word at the top. It says *Quakers*, and the Q is exactly the same as the Q on my necklace.

I say, "What are Quakers?" and perhaps my shock makes me sound angry, because the little girl starts to whimper again.

I say, "Sorry, sorry! I just mean… well, what *are* Quakers? Are you Christians? Do you have crosses? Why were the grown-ups arrested?"

★ ★ ★

Nobody answers me. The little girl stops crying but she seems to huddle down even more into her beanbag. The older two look at each other.

Then the boy says, "Don't you know anything?" He sounds quite angry.

I say, "No, not really. I've never been to school. I'm feckless, you see. Should I know about Quakers?"

The two older kids look at each other again. I know they are still struggling to trust me, and I cannot really blame them.

Then the girl sits down on one of the armchairs and points to another, showing that she wants me to sit down. It is warmer in the hut, not warm but not as cold as outside. I pull the Velcro of my jacket open and it makes a ripping sound, which makes the little girl jump. The boy goes over to the table and switches on an electric kettle. A light on the base comes on. I have never lived in a place with electricity, and I really want to go over and have a look at the kettle, but it is more important that I learn about the Quakers.

The boy says, "Counsellors used to use the children's room during the week, and they left coffee behind. Do you like coffee?"

"Not really," I apologise. "Can I just have hot water?" The boy does not answer. He just goes on making the drinks. When the water is boiling the kettle switches itself off and the light goes out.

He puts the mugs on the little table near to our chairs, and sits down. "Come here, Gracie," he says to the little girl, and she leaves her beanbag and climbs onto his lap. He puts an arm round her and strokes her hair.

The girl says, "Quakers are just people who… we… we're *like* Christians but…"

"I think we *are* Christians," interrupts the boy.

"Well, maybe… yes," agrees the girl. "We listen to the Light within," she says.

"And that's God speaking to us," says the boy. He is drinking his hot drink rather clumsily because of the little girl who is curled up on his lap.

"Yes," agrees the girl. "And we do what we are prompted to do."

"We meet here to worship," says the boy. "We don't call it a church, we call it a meeting house."

"Oh!" I say. "And you call each other *Friends*, so that's why this is called the *Friends' Meeting House!*"

"Yes," agrees the girl. "That's right."

I drink some of my hot water, which is a bit chalky. I can sort of understand how a person might listen to the Light inside themselves, although you would think people would *see* light and *hear* voices. It seems to me that these Quakers are like me. I see colours when other people just hear words.

"Why did they arrest the grown-ups?" I ask.

For a moment neither of them says anything. The girl drinks from her mug and says to the boy, "I really wish we had some milk."

The boy says, "Perhaps Gerald will bring some tomorrow."

The little girl sits up and reaches for her drink. She looks a bit happier now that she is safely on the boy's lap.

The boy says, "We felt it was right to protest about the labour camps."

The girl says, "A group of people went to the South Stockbridge camp and sat on the road outside, so that the trucks carrying the prisoners to the A34 to clear the litter on the hard shoulders couldn't get out of the camp."

"We don't use violence," explains the boy, as if it is very important for me to understand that. "We are always peaceful. But that doesn't make any difference to them!"

"The police?" I ask. "And the anti-terrorists?"

"Yes."

"So they picked them up, off the road, and took them inside the labour camp and made them inmates," says the girl.

The boy says, "But there were only about ten people there. So everyone else wrote letters of protest and we gave out leaflets at the Butter Cross…"

"Then they came to our Sunday Meeting," continues the girl, "and arrested everyone."

"A month ago," says the boy. "They've been gone a month."

I think about their story. I have a nasty feeling. "Will they put you in care?" I ask. "The kids who are left behind?"

The boy gives a worried glance at the little girl on his lap. She is curled up again with the bit of blanket next to her face, her thumb in her mouth and her eyes closed.

"We don't know," he says. "They haven't tried to yet."

The girl says, "One of the Friends, Percy Duxford, used to be a lawyer. He was at Alton when they raided our Meeting, so they didn't arrest him. He's gone to London to try to get everyone free. They didn't break the law."

"They disturbed the peace…" says the boy.

"What, sitting in silence on a road?" says the girl indignantly.

"How many of you are there?" I ask.

"About a dozen, give or take," says the boy. "The twins went to their grandparents, so they're okay. Joey and Matty have an older sister who is looking after them. Percy and his wife took in the three Braithwaite girls. We're not sure what is happening with Harry or Anne-Marie."

"And we can't remember whether Paul and Tina's parents

were at Meeting that day, so we don't know if they were arrested."

"Paul and Tina often came with Joey and Matty," explains the girl.

"And you are living here?" I ask, looking around the little hut again.

"Yeah," agrees the girl.

"Aren't you frightened?" I ask. I'm thinking of the graffiti on the building, of drunk soldiers from the American base coming in at night.

"I am," says the little girl, who I thought was asleep.

"They don't know we're here," says the boy. "We sleep up there," he nods to the balcony bit above our heads.

And the girl says, quite proudly I think, "And on Sundays we have Meeting for Worship in the house. Like the early Quaker children did, when their parents were arrested. Back in the old days. Anyone who wants to, may come!"

"You could come, if you wanted to," says the boy.

★ ★ ★

For a while we talk about their problems. It seems to me as if they are managing quite well. Some people from other churches have brought them food, and the lawyer Percy Duxford has contacted human rights groups in Europe to get them to write lots of letters. There has not been a court case, so the older boy and girl think all the adults will be freed soon. I hope they are right.

Then I look again at the poster of the boy and the girl with their eyes closed, and I say, "So, why are you called Quakers?"

"We just are," says the girl.

The boy says, "There's some story…"

I ask, "Are Quakers always getting into trouble with the police? And with the anti-terrorists?"

161

The girl sounds a bit uncertain. "I think so," she says.

The boy says, "It comes in fits and starts. It's been bad recently."

"Yes," agrees the girl. "Ever since we made that big alliance with America, after we left the European Union. That's when it started to get bad."

The boy says, "Actually, I think Quakers were always running into trouble, right from the time of George Fox. It's sort of in our DNA."

"George Fox?" I say. Actually, I nearly shout it. "*George Fox?*" I ask again. "Who was he?"

The girl looks at me, surprised. "Oh, he lived ages ago," she says.

"Yes, but…" I am thinking about my name, about my parents perhaps naming me after somebody who was important to them.

The boy says, "He sort of started the Quakers."

The little girl, still huddled on her brother's lap, sits up again and says, "No he didn't. We learnt about it in our Meeting. Maria says the Spirit started Quakers."

"Well, yes," says the girl, and shrugs her shoulders, as if to say that this is really not the point.

I take a deep breath. I say, "I think my parents might have been Quakers."

The boy says, "Why don't you ask them?"

"I've lost them," I say, feeling suddenly very sad.

"Well, you never know," says the girl, but I think she is more concerned about the mess they are in, and really I cannot blame them.

I say, "They'll be expecting me back at the…" I stop myself just in time. "At home," I say.

I do up the Velcro on my jacket again. It looks as if it has started raining. It is only early afternoon but already it is getting dark.

The girl says, "Come on Sunday. Come to Meeting for Worship. At eleven o'clock."

I say, "Maybe," and then, "Good luck!" And I head off to the Hill.

★ ★ ★

Vishna, Skye and I talk about the Quakers over our evening meal. Skye seems to know a bit about them, which is a surprise to me because she really isn't religious.

"Oh!" she says, when I first ask her. "Yes, I used to have a friend who was a Quaker. A while ago."

"Aren't you friends anymore?" I want to know. If something made Skye stop being friends with the Quaker she knew, then I'm not sure I want to be friends with people in that group either.

"I would be," she says, "except that she vanished – disappeared. She got on the wrong side of the anti-terrorists. Or maybe she offended someone, I don't know. She was very close to an anti-terrorist officer and I never did trust him."

I want to know about Quakers, not about Skye's friend who has disappeared, even if it is sad for Skye, which I think from her tone of voice it is. I say, "And she was a Quaker, your friend?"

"She certainly was!" says Skye.

Vishna says, "But wasn't it a bit strange, if she was one of the People, that she was friends with an anti-terrorist?"

Skye says, "We all thought so, but they were friends for ages. He obviously had a soft spot for my friend, and for quite a long time I thought he was protecting her. But obviously not, in the end."

"So, what did she believe?" I ask Skye, trying to keep the topic on Quakers.

"Well, that's a good question," says Skye. "She didn't talk

163

much about her religious beliefs at all, although I think she took them very seriously. She went to that Meeting House you discovered on your way home. I'm not surprised that they all got arrested," she adds. "They were never discreet about their opinions. They have this strong attitude to social justice."

Vishna says, "So that's why they brought us food and water."

"I should think so," says Skye, staring into the darkness beyond our fire.

I say, "Skye, if my parents were Quakers, they might have been disappeared too, like your friend."

Skye goes on staring into the darkness, with a little frown on her forehead, and I think she has not heard me, but then she gives a big sigh and looks at me. "Do you know, Giorgi," she says, "I think that that is very likely. Really, very likely."

★ ★ ★

While Vishna and I are jogging up the Hill to get warm before bed, I say to her, "I like to think that my parents were Quakers, because they are good people. And it would explain the cross in the Q."

Vishna says, "I think we ought to go to their Meeting on Sunday, to find out some more. There might be someone there who knew your family." Then she says, puffing a little bit because we jogged fast uphill – you have to, if you want to get really warm – "But I think we ought to talk to Skye again, and the Old Man. It might be a big risk. Skye's friend disappeared, and all the grown-ups at the Quaker Meeting were arrested. Someone really doesn't like those people!"

★ ★ ★

The Old Man likes the idea of us going to the Quaker Meeting better than Skye does. She says, when we talk about it next day, "But, Old Man, the authorities are bound to know that they didn't catch all the children in their net. They'll be watching that Meeting House. It's obvious."

But the Old Man puts his hand on Skye's arm and says, as if I were not there, "The boy needs to know about his roots. Let them go. Nothing in life is without its risks. You should know that!"

He stares into his fire. We are sitting in the big fire circle where the whole community used to gather, close to where the Professor is buried. Then he says to me, "I think you should take that necklace with you. Someone might know about it."

★ ★ ★

When the cathedral clock strikes ten on Sunday morning Vishna and I set off. We are both looking as respectable as possible, because people are out and about on Sunday mornings, having big breakfasts in the city or going to church. As we walk alongside the river Vishna greets people politely with "Good morning," or "A lovely day!" and nobody at all would think we were feckless. It was cold overnight and the grass is white with frost, which is unusual. There are people walking dogs, and a small group of American soldiers runs past us, all panting, wearing heavy-looking backpacks. Everyone gets off the path to let them pass, and some people smile but others frown, and I wonder what they are all thinking. We leave the river path before we get to the bridge, climbing up some steps to a small public garden and then following a little back street to the Friends' Meeting House. I am feeling excited.

When we get there we see that the boy who was in the garden before is squatting a little further along the street, petting a cat. He sees us, glances up and down the street, and when he has seen that there is nobody around he gives a little jerk of his head towards the big wooden gate.

165

"Cool!" says Vishna. "They've got a proper lookout system going."

We go in through the gate and close it quickly behind us. Nobody can see us from the road now unless they go right up to the broken gate and peer through, and I feel safe and excited at the same time. I lead Vishna round the side of the building, expecting to go to the little wooden hut I went into last time. Then a man steps out from the bushes and makes us jump.

"Can I help you?" he asks.

He is quite old, but not really old like the Old Man. He has a grey beard, and he is wearing a cloth cap pulled down over his forehead so that we can barely see his eyes. Vishna says, "We were hoping there might be a Meeting here."

The man says, "What sort of meeting?" He looks at the big house, boarded up at the back, and says, "The Meeting House is closed."

Colours shine in my head as he speaks, the dull orangy-yellow of the word *closed*, but also a much warmer pink colour which is to do with something he has not said but means. It is the colour of *welcome*. I have not seen two colours come at once like this before, and I find it strange.

Vishna hesitates, but I speak up. "Please, sir," I say, being as polite as I can, "we would like to go to a Quaker Meeting."

The man still does not seem convinced. He says, "Why would you want to do that?"

I have a good idea. I fish my symbol of the Q and the cross out from the inside pocket of my snug jacket, and I hold it out to the man. "My parents gave me this," I say. "And they have disappeared. A long time ago."

The man takes the necklace from me and peers at it. Then he takes a pair of glasses out of his pocket and puts them on, and looks more closely at my necklace.

"They were Quakers, weren't they?" I ask, and reach out to take back my symbol.

The man does not hand it back. Instead, he takes off his glasses, looks up at the tall house, then puts them on again and examines my necklace again.

"I have not seen one of these for years," he says. "I don't think many were ever made." He is still looking at my necklace, and then a smile comes slowly all across his face. "If your parents disappeared," he asks, "how did you come to have this?"

To my relief, he hands it back. I put it safely into my inside pocket. "I was wearing it when I was found," I say.

The man frowns. "And the authorities let you keep it?" he queries. "That doesn't sound very likely."

Vishna speaks then. She has been standing still, watching and listening. She says, "He wasn't found by the authorities."

I understand then why the man is suspicious. Of course, if the care people had found me they would have taken my symbol away. I say, "We're Scum of the Earth."

The man looks more confused than suspicious now. He says, "Scum…?"

Vishna laughs. "We're considered feckless," she explains. "We live off-grid."

"Oh, I see!" Now the man looks neither suspicious nor confused, but perhaps a bit surprised. He says, "We're meeting inside today because quite a lot of people are here." He nods to a boarded-up door. "Go on in, and head for the room at the front." He steps back into the bushes, and is gone.

We open the door and find ourselves in a sort of porch area with old fridges and stuff, all with their doors open. It is very quiet. When you live outside it is never completely silent, there are always sounds in the background: wind and birds, the whine of traffic, church bells and aeroplanes, and little creatures skittering through the grass. This complete silence feels a bit creepy to me. We walk through the gloom of a kitchen, past a stairway and into a larger room where chairs are in a circle round a table. On the table there is a candle. They are not using the electric lights, and the room is shadowy. One window is boarded up, the other has newspapers stuck all over it. Nobody can see in and we cannot really see each other until our eyes have adjusted.

At once it reminds me of sitting round the Old Man's fire before everyone went north and the Professor died. There are not crowds of people here, perhaps about twelve. I see the two girls I met before, and several other children round about my own age, but there are grown-ups here too, all sitting very still. Some have their eyes closed; one woman is looking steadily, almost without blinking, at the broken window which has been boarded up; and some are staring at the candle. The flame gives a sort of wriggle because of the breeze we create by coming in and sitting down, but as we settle, so does the flame. People open their eyes and glance at us. Some smile, but others just close their eyes or look away. It feels friendly and peaceful. I look at Vishna. She has shut her eyes, and I wonder what she is doing in her head. I keep my eyes open and look at the candle. For a long while it stays very still, and then it flickers as the man with the cap and the boy from the street come in and sit down. Again, everything goes very still.

I close my eyes too, and then I discover a surprising thing. I am used to words giving me colours in my head, but I do not remember that silence ever did, until today. But with my eyes closed, I can see colours flickering around, the way they might do if the people were talking. Mostly there is a pink colour which flickers to red, the colour of *welcome*, but there is a pretty, soft greyish-blue too, and I see that it is to do with sadness. I think it is coming from the two girls I met before, and I open my eyes and look at them. The little girl is leaning on the bigger girl, and her eyes are closed. She could be asleep. The big girl is looking at the candle and I see that she has tears in her eyes. I understand that she is missing her parents and that, although she has not said the words aloud, in her head she has been talking about them, and I have heard the colours.

The man in the cap, who came in last, stands up. Some people open their eyes and look at him, others do not. After a moment or two, he starts to speak.

"Friends," he says, "on behalf of our little remnant of Winchester Meeting, I welcome you. It is good to see folk from Alton and Andover, and to know that we have your support. In the silence, let us hold in the Light those Winchester Friends who have been so cruelly prevented from being here, and their children. In the silence, let us remember that John said that the Light shines in the darkness, and the darkness cannot put it out."

One or two people sigh, as if acknowledging the truth of what the man has said. I wonder who John was, but I understand that the Light he talked about must be to do with what is good and true, and I feel comforted to think that this John believed that the darkness could not get rid of truth and goodness. Deep inside me, I feel that this is right. I have a sort of feeling that there is a Goodness which is greater than the goodness of Skye, who took me to the camp and saved me from the care people, and greater than the goodness of the Old Man, who kept our camp peaceful and friendly until it was time for most people to go north. I think that perhaps there is a Goodness which is behind everything.

I close my eyes again. More colours are shining in my head. As well as the pink and red of *welcome* there is a golden light, which is the Goodness lying behind all the world, and then the bright green of a new holly leaf, which is also the colour of my dad, and I find myself wondering vaguely why that colour came into my head, but not really caring, because the colours are taking up all my attention and it is as if I am on a ride with them, whirling through the sky.

Then Vishna nudges me, and I come back down to the

dimly lit room and see that everyone is shaking hands and smiling, and one woman is hugging the little girl. I feel as if I have just woken up from a really nice dream. I shake the hands of the people around me, and when everyone has stopped saying, "Good morning!" and "It's good to see you!" we all go quiet again.

The boy stands up. He says, "Thank you, everyone, for coming this morning." He smiles at Vishna and me. "We do not ask visitors to introduce themselves anymore," he says. "Sometimes it is better not to give too much away, but you are very welcome." Then he asks, "Do we have any news of Friends, who wish it given?"

I think that these Quakers speak in a strange and careful way. The cloth-cap man stands and says, "Well, in the last week there have been a few developments in the matter of our arrested Friends. News of the anti-terrorist raid has been circulated in Scotland and Ireland, and the press there is quite interested. All my attempts to find out where they have been taken have drawn a blank, but the Scandinavian papers are reporting that our Friends are in a prison somewhere, all together, and that infants under the age of three have not been taken from their parents. We cannot find that any charges have been laid, but of course that does not mean very much."

A woman asks, looking directly at the boy, "Are you managing?"

It is the girl who answers. She says, "Will and I are okay, but Grace is always frightened and we are worried about her."

They all look at the little girl. She is holding the hand of the big girl and looking at the floor. Cloth-cap man says, "Gracie, do you want to tell us how you are feeling?"

For a moment or so Gracie says nothing, but everyone just waits until she is ready. Then she says in a very quiet voice, "I want my mummy."

People look at each other in a sad sort of way. An elderly man with a walking stick says, without standing up, "Will, Pixie and Gracie, Maria and I have a suggestion to make to you, after this Meeting."

The boy, Will, stands up again. "Do we have any other notices?" he asks. I think that Will is very young to be in charge, not even as old as Big Bear, but then, if all the adults have been arrested…

Someone talks about a demonstration the United Socialists are going to have in London against the detentions of activists, and someone else tells us that Walker is out of hospital and doing well, and he sends us all his love. Then cloth-cap man stands again and says, "Friends, there will be tea and coffee in the kitchen and of course everyone is welcome to stay. I should warn you, though, that a Swedish journalist has asked to speak to some of us for an article she is writing, and she expects to arrive here by one o'clock. So, for those who do not wish to risk a journalist, please be sure that you are out of the way before then!" There are a few laughs and grunts of approval. Then cloth-cap man adds, "And I'm sure I don't need to remind you that we need to leave a few at a time, and only when the coast is clear."

The boy Will adds, "Pixie will give you a signal, won't you?" and Pixie nods and smiles.

* * *

I expect that Vishna will want to go quite soon, but she starts talking to cloth-cap man and a younger woman who tells us she is from Alton. I eat three cookies, and out of the corner of my eye I see the woman Maria hugging Gracie again, and the man who is with Maria says, "Good, that's settled, then!" And I realise that Will, Pixie and Gracie are going to go and live in their house for a while. I feel pleased. Their

171

little wooden hut does not seem like a safe place to me.

Vishna says to me, "Hey, Giorgi, do you think this Swedish journalist is the same one Skye was talking to?"

I wonder the same thing. Vishna says, "We could stay here and see for ourselves," and I forget altogether that she might recognise me from when I crept up on her in the nature reserve, so I say, "Okay."

And as soon as she comes in she does recognise me! She says, sounding really surprised, "Edward! It is Edward Pearson, isn't it?" and she holds out her hand to shake mine.

Vishna looks really, really surprised. I never did tell Skye or Vishna about that creeping up thing, and of course my name is not Edward Pearson. It makes me feel a bit odd, as if I have been caught out in a lie.

I say, "Hi, Mrs Saker!" and hold out my hand to shake hers, because it is what the journalist expects. Vishna is giving me a funny look, but she does not say anything.

Vishna says, "Do you know a friend of ours? Skye?"

The journalist looks even more surprised. She says, "Why, yes!" Then she looks at my jacket, and says, "So it was you I bought that parka for!"

It is not really a parka, because parkas have fur hoods and are old-fashioned, but I do not tell her that. I just say, "Oh, thank you!"

"So, how do you guys know Skye?" asks Liliane Saker, the journalist.

Of course, we do not give away that sort of information, so Vishna just says, "It's a long story," and the journalist understands, and says, "Right!"

Then cloth-cap man says, "It might be best if we go upstairs to talk," and the few of us who are left climb the dark, creaking, wooden stairs to a room which seems to be a disused bedroom. It is not the one with the open window and the blowing curtain I saw last time. We sit on the bed, which has a mattress and two pillows but no sheets or blankets, and on a wicker chair, and on the floor.

Cloth-cap man says to the journalist, "Thank you for coming, Liliane," and the journalist says, "It's my privilege," and then we all settle down to what seems to be the business of the Meeting.

The journalist explains what I already know – that she is Swedish, that she has been placed at the School of Journalism at Winchester University, and that she is interested in people she calls 'dissidents'. She talks about her commitment to human rights, and then she comes to the interesting bit.

She says, "It is very difficult, actually, to get any information about what is going on from the authorities here, but my husband back in Sweden has contacts. He thinks the Winchester Quakers have been incarcerated all together, in one prison, as you were told, I believe, earlier today. They are not in the capital, in London, as far as we can tell, so they must be out in the provinces somewhere. There are some jails we can rule out because we have inside information in those institutions, but there are a lot of prisons in England, as you know. There have been a number of protests about the arrests – demonstrations outside English embassies in at least a dozen European cities, to say nothing of India and Costa Rica, and Canada naturally. Of course, these protests have not been reported here. The Canadians are threatening sanctions. We are hoping that if we keep the pressure on, your people will be released, but it is not a forgone conclusion."

The younger woman, who is sitting on the floor, asks, "Have you heard any news of anyone by name?" Then she adds, "My sister was arrested. She's pregnant."

The journalist looks sorry. "No," she says, "no names. But we think there is someone involved in prison transportation leaking information to a group in France, and from him or her we gather that there have been no large-scale transports out of the country, so we can be pretty sure they are not in Cuba, or on their way to the new set-up in Puerto Rica. We hope – and believe – that they are just incarcerated."

"*Just* incarcerated!" queries the woman on the floor.

"I'm sorry," says the journalist. "I didn't mean to minimise your troubles. But incarceration alone shouldn't harm your sister too much, whereas rendition or hard labour…"

Cloth-cap man says, "Let's hold all our Friends in the Light again, and those who risk so much to try to help us." He smiles at the journalist, to show that he is including her. Then he reminds us all, "And please leave carefully. Pixie won't be outside anymore, and we really don't want people guessing that the Meeting House is still in use."

After another silence, a blue-grey one this time, we feel our ways through the dim light of the stairwell. Just as she reaches the bottom step the journalist turns and looks up at Vishna and me. We are on the half landing above. She says, "I don't suppose you are called Edward Pearson at all, are you?" But before I can answer Vishna says, "It's as good a name as any."

The journalist considers for a moment, then says, "Yes, it is a good name, as names go." She is buttoning up her coat ready to leave, but just as she is going through into the kitchen she says, quite casually, "I still like to walk in the nature reserve. There are so few people there at this time of the year. It gives me a clear head, so that I can think." Then she goes.

While we wait for cloth-cap man to tell us it is safe for us to leave too, Vishna says to me, "I think you have a story to tell me, *Edward Pearson!*"

★ ★ ★

I tell them all, Vishna, Skye and the Old Man, as we eat our evening meal round our fire when it is dark. It is Skye's last night before going on another trip. She hopes for further news of those who have gone north, and she will tell us all about it. She thinks she will be back by Christmas, if not before. Vishna says, when she hears about me creeping up on the journalist, "Wow, Giorgi, you took a real risk there!" and Skye looks worried, but the Old Man says, talking about me as if I were not there, "But the boy needs to be able to stand on his own two feet, and he came to no harm."

Then he looks directly at me, and says, "Your search has come a long way, hasn't it, since we last had a discussion?"

"It has," I agree.

"So, tell us where you think you have got to," he suggests.

I pause for a moment. Then I say, "Well, I know that the People are called Quakers and that the Q and the cross was a Quaker symbol, so I think my parents were Quakers." I stop and think about that, and correct my statement. "*Are* Quakers," I say. "And I think they were... are, good people, and that they were arrested, and perhaps they are doing hard labour, or have been sent to some place abroad, or maybe they are just incarcerated, and that is why I lost them." I stop and think about that, and then I say, "Perhaps the working hypothesis about my name needs to be changed now. Do you think I might have been called after George Fox, who started the Quakers?"

"Now, that's a good question," says the Old Man.

Vishna says, "It's beginning to seem more likely than you being named after George Harrison."

Skye says, "It doesn't really matter, though, Giorgi, does it? Whether you were named after someone who was famous or someone your parents loved, or whether they just liked the name, you can be pretty sure their reasons were good, because they were good people."

"Yes," I say, and I feel comfortable, and I realise, too, that the Old Man has stopped Vishna or Skye from telling me off about the journalist and the nature reserve.

Altogether I feel warm and happy when I climb into my sleeping bag, even though Skye will probably be gone when I wake up in the morning, and even though I still have not actually found my parents. For a few minutes, before I go to sleep, I think about the colours I saw in the silence of the Meeting, of how they moved and changed and were beautiful. Just as I am going to sleep I say to the golden light, "Don't let me grow out of this!"

And then I wake up, and it is morning.

CHAPTER 4

The Song

For a few days after the Quaker Sunday, Vishna and I spend our time just catching up on routine activities. Our woodpile needs restocking, and we have to go quite a long way, down the Hill towards the river, to find decent sticks that won't flare up and then burn in two minutes flat. We have to wait until dark to fill up our water bottles from the tap in the garden of the cottage by the school, and we have clothes to wash. Drying them is difficult, because the weather is damp, and we don't want to hang them by the fire because, as Vishna says, if we walk into the city smelling of smoke it will be a dead giveaway. We need to do some food gleaning too, and with only the two of us we are a bit concerned. The man at the fruit stall gives us parsnips and tangerines, but we need a more varied diet than that.

Fortunately there is some sort of conference at the hotel by the cathedral, and one night in the middle of the week Vishna comes up the Hill with unopened packets of sandwiches and biscuits that have not even reached their sell-by date, and for one night a stranger visits the Old Man. We do not meet the stranger, but the following evening the Old Man invites us to eat our evening meal with him at the big fire circle, and we eat a rich, tasty stew which the Old Man tells us is hare. I cannot go into the city during the day because it is no longer half term, but in the evenings everything is lit up. They have hung the Christmas decorations across the streets, but they haven't turned the lights on yet. They will do that in time for

Thanksgiving, which is an American festival which is big in England too, now that we are in the New Alliance. There are a lot of festivals at this time of year. Big Bear, Little Bear, Limpy and I used to love it, and it is a surprise to me to think that this time last year Vishna had not even joined us yet.

The best of the festivals, from our point of view, is Bonfire Night. The people in the city have a big celebration on the nearest Saturday, with a procession through Winchester with everyone carrying burning torches, and a huge fire in the park where Skye once told me there used to be a camp of homeless people. For days before and after the Saturday celebration, people have little bonfires and small firework displays in their back gardens, but the best fireworks are always on the Saturday. Ever since I can remember we have sat on the earthworks and watched it all. "The best seats in town!" said Skye once.

This year there is just Vishna and me. We sit on the earthworks where our camp used to be, looking out over the city. The river looks black and a little shiny, winding its way through the water meadows a long way below us. We cannot see the procession from here, we are too far round, but once the fireworks start, shooting up into the air with hisses and bangs and exploding in pinks and blues and greens, we can see everything. For a little while we just say to each other the things people always say, like, "Wow! That was a good one!" and, "Hey! Look at that!" Then, while a fountain of sparks flies up into the air like a waterfall, changing from orange to green and back to orange again, Vishna says, "Shall we go to the Quaker Meeting again tomorrow?"

I am glad she has asked. I say, "I would like to."

Vishna says, "They are your people, in a way, aren't they?"

I watch a big rocket whistling up into the air, even higher than us, and then exploding into white and gold stars, and I do not say anything for a few minutes. I am thinking about the colours I could see last Sunday as we sat in silence, and I say, "I sort of fit in there."

"Yes," says Vishna, "I think you do."

★ ★ ★

The lookouts in the street the next morning are two oldish-looking ladies. They are standing under an umbrella with the stars and stripes on it, because it is pouring with rain, and they just look like two ladies who have met by accident in the street. We do not even realise they are lookouts until one woman glances up and down the street, waits for a boy with a dog to go along the path by the children's play area, and then gives us the thumbs-up sign.

I recognise some of the faces from the week before. The man with the cloth cap is sitting in the far corner, and next to him is the journalist. There is a young couple I did not see last week, with a sleeping baby. Vishna and I are just settling into our seats when Will, Pixie and Gracie come in, with the people who are looking after them. They see us, and smile. Even Gracie smiles, and I think that after just one week of being looked after by grown-ups she is feeling happier.

I find it much harder to find my way into the Meeting this week. I close my eyes, and I expect to see the colours whirling around, as they did the week before, but it is just ordinary, the way it is when I close my eyes at night and can only hear the wind in the trees, and no talking. I think about the golden light, which is the Goodness which lies behind all the world, and I think I can see it, but I am not sure. Perhaps I just see the memory of it. But I do feel a sort of stillness in my mind, and that is good, a sort of calm, the way it is very early on a summer morning if you wake up just as it starts to get light, before all the birds have started singing.

Singing.

Singing.

The word *singing* seems to go around in my head. Then the words I half remember from the days before I lost my parents, the words of the song, *How can I keep from singing?*

I feel a sort of shock going through me, and I open my eyes. Cloth-cap man is looking directly at me, a thoughtful sort of expression on his face. I feel a sort of panic. I think that I must have made a noise, or moved suddenly. But the man just gives me a big smile and closes his eyes again. I look at the candle which is burning steadily on the table, and I listen to the little sucking noises the baby is making on its dummy, and my heart starts to beat slow and steady again. I close my eyes, but my mind is busy. I think, *I mustn't ignore the last clue. I must find out about the songs too.* Then at last I can see the golden light of the Goodness, but it is a long way away and not as bright as last week. Never mind, it is there.

Nobody speaks during the Meeting, until just before the end. Then Gracie starts to wriggle and move around in her chair, so that I think perhaps she needs the loo. Then she stands up and says in her quiet little voice, "Take heed, dear Friends, to the prompting of love and truth in your hearts…" Then she just stands there for a few minutes, and sits down again. I see Pixie reach over and give her a sort of quick hug.

I think, *Is the golden light prompting me to think about those songs? Is that what I need to do next? Did the golden light put that idea into my head?* Then I think that I do not want to talk to Vishna or to Skye about this, or even the Old Man. It sounds like an odd thing to say, but I want to do this on my own, just me and the golden light.

★ ★ ★

Will does the announcements at the end, again, and thanks the people from Andover and Alton for coming over to join us.

He says that there is tea and coffee in the kitchen, and we all troop through. It seems that Will, Pixie and Gracie have been making muffins with Maria, who is looking after them, and we all tuck in happily. They are soft and gooey in the middle, and taste of chocolate.

Vishna is talking to the journalist. She is telling Vishna that she is a Muslim, and that she too tries to listen to the promptings of love and truth. Will says to me, "Do you want to come with us into the children's room?"

Other than the baby, who does not really count, Will and his sisters and I are the only children here this week. I say, "Okay," and we run through the pouring rain to the little hut.

It is pretty much the same as when I last saw it. Will says, "I want to get some of my stuff," and he starts to climb the ladder to get up to the sleeping platform. "Come and see!" he says, so I follow him up.

It is a bit of a mess up here. The three sleeping bags are all muddled up, the way they must have been when Will, Pixie and Gracie last wriggled out of them, and there are items of clothing scattered around. It is cosy, though, and I think perhaps the children had been safer than I had realised. It feels very hidden and secret. I watch Will bundling up this and that and pushing them into a cloth bag, but he does not touch the sleeping bags.

"Don't you need those?" I ask.

Will says, "No, we sleep in proper beds at Maria's."

Then I think, *I wonder if I have ever slept in a proper bed?* I have seen pictures of them, in books, and there is a shop in St George's Street that sells them, and I have looked in the window and thought how big they are, and how far off the ground. I want to ask Will if he ever falls out of his proper bed, but I do not want to look ignorant, so I do not say anything else.

When he has gathered up everything he wants, Will says to me, "So, is your name Edward?"

181

"Not really," I say, but I don't tell him what it actually is.

"I'm called Will," he says, which of course I know now. I think he is inviting me to tell him my real name, but I don't. Instead I ask, "Are your parents feckless?"

"What?" asks Will, as if I have said something he does not understand.

"Scum of the Earth," I try to explain.

He just looks blankly at me. I try again, "Does your dad have a job?" I ask. "Do you go to school?"

Now he understands. "Oh," he says. "Dad is an accountant. Self-employed. And Mum is an illustrator. And we go to school in Harestock. Or we do when we're not at Maria's."

I do not know about people being self-employed. It seems like an odd idea. Does Will's father pay himself for doing work? And if so, where does the money come from? I think I will ask Skye when she comes back in time for Christmas. Or maybe the Old Man.

Will says, "So, are you and that girl going to come to Meeting every week?"

We are sitting on the rumpled sleeping bags, and I realise we are becoming friends. I say, "Well, perhaps. Probably. I hope so."

Will says, "You said your parents might have been Quakers."

"Yes," I agree. I take my cross in the Q out of my inside pocket and pass it to Will. He looks at it carefully. I explain, "I was wearing it when S…" I stop just in time. "When I was found."

"It's our Q, all right," says Will. "But it's odd that it has a cross in it. We don't usually go for crosses."

Then Will gives me a big, friendly smile. "I think they were Quakers, your mum and dad, so I think you should become a Quaker too. You and that girl. It's fun. We do all sorts of stuff." Then he looks serious and adds, "Well, anyway, we do if our parents aren't being arrested!"

★ ★ ★

When we go back into the main house most people have gone. Vishna and the man with the cloth cap, who is called Percy, and the journalist, Liliane, are talking together, and all the muffins have gone. Maria is sitting on a chair in the dark little room which leads off the kitchen, with Gracie on her lap. I do not see Pixie anywhere.

Percy sees us coming in, and says, "Oh, there you are, boys," and it feels friendly, the way it was when Walking Tall talked to Little Bear and me. Then he says, "Has Will explained anything about our Meetings?"

I think Will looks a little ashamed, so I quickly say, "I have been asking him other things." Then I add, "Gracie stood up and said those words which are on the wall in the children's room."

For a moment Percy looks blank, then he says, "Oh! I see! You mean when she spoke in Meeting. It was brave of her, wasn't it?"

I think about standing up in front of several adults and saying words from a poster, and I think of how fearful Gracie usually seems to be, and I agree. "It was," I say. "Very brave."

"We call it *ministry*," says Percy. "It is when the Spirit gives someone words to say."

"The Spirit is the Goodness?" I ask.

Percy pauses for a moment, then he smiles. "That's a pretty good way of explaining it, actually. The Spirit is the Goodness."

So then I know that although I did not see all the colours this time, the way I did the week before, the Goodness has spoken to me, first with an idea and then with Gracie's words.

I say to Percy, "I think I need to become a Quaker."

Percy laughs out loud. "Whoa! Whoa!" he says, as if I am a horse. "There's no hurry." Then perhaps I look disappointed, because he says, "Of course, the choice is mostly yours in the end. But give it a few more weeks."

★ ★ ★

One thing is bothering me. As we walk up the Hill I say to Vishna, "You never hear the Quakers singing, do you?"

Vishna stops and looks at me, a puzzled expression on her face. "People don't sing much, do they?" she says. "I mean, not while they're having coffee or chatting to people." She giggles. "Wouldn't it be funny," she says, "if someone just burst out into song? Like a musical."

I think she is talking about movies, but I have never seen one. I say, "Yes, but in their Meetings."

We have got to the place on the Hill where the well-worn track fades away into a patch of mud. From this point onwards we try to use different routes up to our shelters, so that people walking their dogs do not think there is a footpath and follow it, and discover us. I go right, a way which begins to go back down the Hill, then jump over a bare patch of ground into some tall grass that makes my legs wet, then sharp left and along and up. Vishna follows me. As we round the corner of the Hill towards the motorway the wind hits us with a splatter of rain in its breath, and Vishna pulls up her hood.

When we are walking side by side again she says, "They sing in other churches. Hymns and chants. But the Quakers hardly even talk, do they?"

"They talk a lot when they're not in a Meeting," I point out. Then I add, "We used to sing a lot before all the others went north. And do you remember the Music Maker? He used to go up the Hill and sing, to sort out his spirit."

We walk along together, thinking about it all. I am wondering whether perhaps my parents were not Quakers after all, because I can remember those two parts of songs, and then I wonder whether my memory is reliable. Vishna is obviously thinking about something else, because she says, "I miss them, the others. Do you?"

Then I feel a little guilty, because I would like to play with Little Bear, and talk to him and all the other kids about everything we have seen and done since they left, but as long as Vishna and the Old Man are here and Skye keeps coming back to check on us, I feel fine. I do not feel as if I should say, "No, I don't miss them!" but I don't want to tell a lie and say, "Yes," so instead I say, "I wonder what they are doing right now."

We can see a thin wisp of smoke now, from our fire, or maybe from the hearth by the Old Man's shelter, and Vishna changes the subject. She says, "Shall we have hot soup for our snack, with those croissants I picked up yesterday? And I have these." She pulls two rather squashed muffins out of her pocket, and my tummy rumbles, although Vishna will not be able to hear it over the groaning wind and the creaking trees.

★ ★ ★

Some time passes. Time is a mysterious thing, because you cannot stop it. Everything else in this world you can stop if you want to badly enough: we could stop the traffic if we put big pieces of wood on the road; we could stop the river from flowing if we dammed it up; but the things that belong to time you cannot stop. Growing belongs to time. My feet are growing all the time and my new trainers are pinching, and my hair is growing so that Vishna takes her scissors to it and cuts it short like the hair of the boys who hang around the

Guildhall. And the days are passing and no one can stop them, even if they wanted to.

Down in the city there is a big Thanksgiving celebration, which all the shops seem to be advertising even though it is an American festival, not ours at all. Vishna and the Old Man decide to have a little Thanksgiving of our own, for giving thanks for our freedom and for the others getting safely into Scotland, and for our health, and for the Hill and for each other. Vishna gleans some pieces of chicken and we cook them over the fire in the big fire circle, on sticks. It is wet and windy again, but not too bad in the shelter of the trees. I remember when there was a big crowd of us on the Hill, and we used to sit round this same fire circle, talking and singing until us kids were almost asleep. I say to the Old Man and Vishna, "Shall we sing a song?" But Vishna says, "It won't be the same without the others." I know she is right, so instead we play a game, trying to say the name of a country for each letter of the alphabet. I have become quite good at this since the time Skye brought back the atlas last summer, but I do not know a country which begins with X.

I am feeling thankful nearly all the time, now. It is easier to wander around Winchester when it is dark so much. I often go down when the light starts to turn from the grey of daytime to the blue of dusk, and I walk up and down the High Street looking at the brightly lit market stalls. There is a Christmas market in the cathedral close, with ice skating on ice which they have to make with a machine because it is not cold enough for anything to freeze. Mostly it is wet, but my jacket keeps me warm and dry and well disguised. One day I find a shiny dollar coin on the ground by the fruit man's stall, and I say to him, "Is this yours?" and hold it out to him in my open hand.

He says, "You are a good kid; you can keep it." He gives me a bag full of tangerines and a box which has dates in it. He says, "Don't eat the dates all at once; they'll give you tummy ache!" I take the dollar to the stall that sells bread, and buy a small loaf of brown, seedy bread which I know we will all like. The woman at the bread stall says, "Oh, I'll throw in one of these, too, because it is the end of the day." She doesn't do any throwing, though. She just passes me a paper bag, and when I look inside there is a cake with icing on it, wrapped up in plastic. I say, "Thank you very much!" and walk quickly away before she can change her mind.

I think about how kind people are, and then I suddenly seem to notice: there are no beggars anymore. I wonder what the police have done with them. I expect that they are in labour camps, and I hope they have not been given hard labour, because when they talked about hard labour at the Quaker Meeting it sounded bad, like care.

For several Sundays, Vishna and I walk down the Hill together and go to the Quaker Meeting. Usually there are just a few people. I never see as many as I saw that first Sunday, and I realise that it is because most of the children who belong to the Meeting are living with other Quakers now, in Alton or Andover, or perhaps in Southampton. Will, Pixie and Gracie come every Sunday; Maria drives them over. Percy is nearly always there, although he is still fighting to get the grown-ups out of prison and sometimes this fighting takes him up to London, which is our capital city and the place where our king lives when he is not in Washington DC. Actually, I discover, the Quakers do not really fight at all, not in the sense of hitting people or pushing people over earthworks. It is one of the many reasons for the authorities not liking them. They refuse to take part in the war in the Caribbean, and instead suggest ways of making peace, which annoys the government. Percy tries to explain it to me one Sunday. He says, "There is a lot of money to be made out of war," and that mystifies me, because I think war mostly consists of blowing people up or leaving them hungry. But

Percy is a very clever man, a retired lawyer, as well as being kind, so if he says war makes people rich it must be true, even though I cannot understand how this can be.

Will, Pixie and Gracie are going to school near to Maria's house. She registered them there, and they say it is pretty good. None of the remaining Quakers are feckless, so they can all send their children to school, and go to the doctor if they are ill, and show their papers to the police if they are stopped.

Will and I become mates. He knows my real name now, and says, "Hi, Giorgio!" whenever we walk into the Meeting House kitchen. Every Sunday after Meeting we go to the children's room and sit upstairs in the sleeping area and talk. Sometimes Pixie comes too. We guess that Will is about a year older than me and Pixie perhaps a bit younger, and she is a cool girl, with the same sort of sense that Vishna has. They ask Maria to drive them over to Winchester every Sunday because they want to keep the Meeting open until the grown-ups come back. Some people from other Meetings come most Sundays, just one or two, to help support Winchester, and the journalist usually comes. She is a Muslim, but she likes to sit in silence with us.

One morning when we arrive there is a sort of excitement in the air. When I sit down in the circle and close my eyes I can see the fizzing yellow of people's silent words to the Goodness. Gradually, as the hour passes, the yellow stops fizzing and becomes smooth and golden, like the Goodness itself, and soft, gentle colours swirl in, and it is like the colours I used to see around the fire circle when all the shelters were on the Hill and we sang songs together. I think that although the Quakers do not sing with their voices, they sing with their spirits.

Afterwards, during the notices, I find out what the joy is all about. Will or Pixie always seem to be in charge. One or other of them always asks whether there are any notices, but it seems to me that if Percy is there he does the job of backing them up. He is here this morning, looking happy. When Pixie asks if there are any notices, and nobody else has said anything, Percy stands up and speaks.

He says, "Well, Friends, some of you will already know... Our friend Liliane has had her article published – the article she came here hoping to write." He picks up a newspaper from under the chair where he was sitting. It is in Swedish. Percy says, "It has attracted a lot of interest right through the European Union, and a translation has been published in the Canadian papers. And here," he picks up another newspaper, "is the same translated article in today's Scottish papers!"

Quakers seem to like to do things in quite an orderly way, but all the grown-ups (there are seven that day) lean forward in their chairs and I think someone might grab the article. Nobody does, though. Percy goes on, "Now that the arrest of our Friends is so widely known, we are hoping that the authorities will be embarrassed enough to release them. My colleagues in Belgium and I are working to get them home by Christmas."

When we have heard some other news, and Pixie has reminded us that there are drinks in the kitchen, everyone gathers round Liliane the journalist and shakes her hand, or hugs her, or both, and the spoken words of everyone make the same fizzy and excited yellow in my head as I saw during the silence.

I have not thought, until today, how close Christmas is. There will be one more Sunday, and then Christmas Day comes during the following week. When there were lots of children in the camp we used to make little presents for each other. I used to have a pipe that played five notes, that the Music Maker made for me. This year I have not prepared at all, and I feel a bit guilty. Still, there is time.

When Will, Pixie and I are sitting in the children's room,

Pixie says to me, "What will you and Vishna do on Christmas Day?"

I say, "I'm not sure." I am thinking that I hope Skye comes back. If Will's and Pixie's parents come home, and Skye returns to the Hill, we will all be reunited with our best people. Except, of course, that I still have not found my mum and dad…

★ ★ ★

I am beginning to understand what people mean when they talk about praying. In fact, grown-up Quakers do not talk about it much at all; they say things like, "We must hold Walker in the Light," or, "Let us remember the people of the Caribbean." But Pixie and Will talk about praying, a bit, once they know me enough to discuss important stuff. Pixie says, "I have prayed for Mum and Dad every day since they were arrested," and Will once told me, "When you pray you are asking for love to take over." I remember that the man John told people that Light is stronger than darkness and that darkness cannot put out the Light, and in my mind I think that if the Light were a person, praying would be a bit like holding hands with the Light.

When there are grown-ups you really trust, like Skye, and even Vishna, who is nearly grown-up, sometimes you are walking along and you just find yourself holding hands with them. If you had to think, *When did we start holding hands?* you cannot remember, because it just came naturally while you were talking, or looking at the swans flying, or whatever was going on at the time. And you do not know whether you reached for their hand, or they reached for yours.

I think I do that sort of praying on the way back up the Hill. The sort of praying which is like holding hands without noticing you are. My prayer is that Skye really will be back for Christmas, and when we turn the corner by the scrubby blackberry bushes, where we first catch a glimpse of our shelter, there is Skye, poking the fire and doing something with the can we hang over the flames when we are cooking.

I call, "Skye!" and run up the last few steps, and she stands up and gives me a big hug, and then she says, "Giorgi! It isn't possible! I've only been away a few weeks and look how you've grown!"

Then she hugs Vishna too, and says, "You look great. How's it going?"

★ ★ ★

We spend all afternoon catching up on our news. We cannot comfortably sit still because of the wet wind, so we pull our hoods up over our heads and walk all the way round the Hill, below the copse. When we get to the place where all the shelters used to be, we see that almost all the signs we left are vanishing. Really all that remains is the paddling pool which still does not have water in it, and the ditches we dug round the tents and the huts to stop the rain pouring in, and even they have become more shallow and have started to fill up with dead leaves and other bits and pieces of nature.

We stand on the earthworks and look down on the river and the city. It is a grey and misty afternoon and Winchester, which sometimes feels quite close, looks a long way away. The cathedral bells are ringing for something special but they, too, sound as if they belong somewhere else, and it seems as if there is just we three and the Old Man in all the world. And of course, the Goodness, but you cannot see that.

Skye has already been shown the Swedish newspaper article and the Canadian translation which has been published in Scotland. "And Ireland," says Skye. The journalist Liliane is going home for Christmas, and Skye says, "They will never let her back into this country again, of course," and Vishna chuckles. I feel a bit sad about it, but also a little relieved, because I cannot forget that I lied to her, and it makes me feel uncomfortable that she knows that and I know that.

In the evening we join the Old Man at the big fire circle, and drink bitter tea, and Vishna tells Skye about my comment that the Quakers do not sing.

The Old Man says, "Well, they probably do. People sing when they're happy, whoever they are."

Then Vishna and Skye decide to teach me some songs which belong to this time of the year. I already know 'Jingle Bells' and 'It's a Hap-Hap-Happy Christmas' because we used to sing them in the camp, but now they teach me religious songs, and the Old Man does not mind because there are no longer other people around to make difficulties if we talk (or sing) about religion. Vishna wants to teach me 'Away in a Manger' but Skye says I am already too old for that, and so I learn 'In the Bleak Midwinter', and when we get to the bit about, *Yet, what can I give him, poor as I am?* I feel sad, because perhaps we four are quite poor, with just our shelters and the clothes on our backs. Then we sing, *Yet what I can I give him, give my heart.* I think that we are singing about the Goodness, which is more than a him or a her, but which is definitely a real Being, and to which we will, all four, give our hearts. It makes tears come into the corners of my eyes.

The Old Man has a good voice for singing, and so does Vishna. I find it more difficult to keep to the tune but I do not think the others mind. Then I say, taking a risk, "Do you know a song about *How can I keep from singing?* or *Bed is too small for my tired head."?* But they do not.

192

Vishna says, "Sing them to us," but of course I cannot, because I only know little bits of them.

Even so, when we all go to bed that night I am feeling happy and as if everything is going right.

★ ★ ★

We celebrate our Christmas on the Hill. Skye has brought gifts, and the Old Man, who I cannot remember giving gifts before, has made a wind chime for Vishna and me, to hang outside our shelter. It has hollow pieces of wood of different lengths hanging from a roundish bit of thick bark, with a snail's shell hanging in the middle. When the shell catches the wind, the wooden bits make a sort of bonging noise, each hanging piece a different note. The Old Man says, "I hope it won't keep you awake at night!" But I know that it will not. The sound of the wind chime will make us think of the Old Man. It will be no more disturbing than hearing Vishna on the other side of the curtain.

My gift from Skye is a book called *Swallows and Amazons*. She says, "I used to love that book when I was your age."

So I say, "How old am I?"

And Skye says, "About the right age to read *Swallows and Amazons*." And we all laugh.

I have made carved pictures for the others, to put outside the shelters. I got the idea from thinking about people putting crosses outside their church buildings to tell people what goes on inside. I carve *OM* on the Old Man's sign and *V* on the piece of wood to hang outside the shelter where Vishna and I live, but I have carved the complete word *Skye* on Skye's gift, partly because she has always been so special to me and partly because I made her present first and I still thought I had lots of time. Vishna has made her gifts too. We each have necklaces made of acorns and bits of wood, and we all put them on at once and tell each other how good we look. We have quite ordinary food out of tins, because the best Christmas gleaning comes the day after the festival, but it is a happy time. We sit round the big fire circle and sing 'In the Bleak Midwinter' and some other religious songs that the others know from days gone by, as well as the usual songs we used to sing when everyone was here. We even sing 'The Tax Man' and laugh a lot, and Skye tells us that in Scotland Christmas is not a big deal, and that the big celebrations all happen at the New Year.

It starts to get dark soon after the cathedral clock has struck four. After weeks of damp winds and flurries of rain, the air has turned colder and we can already see the moon. The Old Man says he will stay by the fire and stir the soup, but Skye, Vishna and I walk down to the earthworks to watch the valley getting dark. Vishna says, "If Percy is right, the Quaker adults should be home by now."

Then Skye says, "I hope they're not banking on that. You never know, with the authorities."

I say, "Gracie is longing for her mum to come back. She says so every Sunday."

"I expect they all are," suggests Skye. Then I think of Will, Pixie and Gracie telling their parents what has been happening while they were in prison, and I wonder what it will be like if I ever meet my parents again. There will be such a lot to say. Will we ever be able to catch up with each other? Skye notices a change in me each time she comes back, and she is usually only gone a few weeks. My parents have not seen me since I was a really little guy. It will be odd for them, and odd for me too.

Vishna says, "The stars are shining. Look!" We have not seen stars for weeks because of the drizzle and the clouds. So we identify the different constellations and talk about light pollution and how you cannot really see many stars if you are in the city until they turn off the street lights at midnight.

★ ★ ★

Skye is gone again by the next Sunday. She just made a short visit to celebrate Christmas with us, but she does some useful stuff while she is here. She discovers that I have outgrown my trainers already, and gleans me a new pair. She gleans me a pair of jeans, too, long trousers to wear on cold days if I want to go into the city, because boys who are not feckless do not wear shorts when the weather gets really cold. It feels odd to have my legs covered, and I do not really like it, but I know how important it is to blend in. Skye helps Vishna and me to stock up our woodpile too, and spends time talking to the Old Man, by his shelter, where Vishna and I have never been.

She leaves on the Saturday after Christmas, saying that when she returns she hopes she will have first-hand information about how Little Bear and his family are getting on. Then I know that this time Skye is going right into Scotland, and I wonder if she has ever done that before.

On Sunday we walk down the Hill by a new way, to the old towpath and into the city, to go to the Quaker Meeting. We are used to it now, but if you try to look at the building the way a stranger might, you can see that it looks abandoned and disused. Pixie is keeping watch, standing by the path through to the children's play area. Nobody else is around. It is a cold day, and I am wearing my long trousers for the first time and feeling a bit self-conscious. We catch Pixie's eye, and I think she looks sad, not like a girl whose parents have just come home, but she gives us a nod and we go in.

I expect the meeting room to be full today, because of all the grown-ups who have come home, but it is just the same people as usual. When I sit down and close my eyes I find it hard to concentrate because I am wondering in my head what has gone wrong. Bit by bit, though, the Meeting settles down, and the colours start to come. They are only sad colours: greys and pale blues and a wavy sort of green. In my heart I try to reach out for the golden light, the Light which cannot be put out by darkness, but it is hard work. There is too much sadness in the room.

After quite a long time, Maria stands up. Usually if people are going to say something in Meeting they first stand and then speak, but Maria just stands, not saying anything, for what seems like quite a long time. Then she just says an odd thing, "The Lord has turned my weeping into joy." She sits down again. I think, *What does that mean?* But I do notice that whatever it means, the colours in the room start to change. There is a gentle pink colour, winding itself around the grey.

Then we hear the big wooden gate opening. Immediately everyone has his or her eyes open. For a moment, I am sure, we all think that there is going to be a raid.

Gracie shouts, "Mummy!" and runs to the front door, which cannot be opened, and then runs the other way, out to the kitchen.

A whole crowd of people come in through the gate. There are men and women, and two of the women and one of the men are carrying little ones in their arms. In the meeting room everyone starts to talk and laugh, and there is a bustle of people at the door to the kitchen, all wanting to meet the newcomers. Some grown-ups are crying. Even Vishna is crying, and we do not know these people!

It is like when we used to have birthday parties up on the Hill. People spill out into the small, dark room at the front of the building and stand talking and laughing in the kitchen, and in the meeting room itself, which is usually so quiet. Everyone seems to be hugging everyone else. Gracie has been picked up by a tall man with dark rings under his eyes and a pair of glasses with one piece of glass cracked, and a woman is stroking Pixie's hair and talking to Percy. Will is getting more mugs out of a cupboard. We were not expecting this many people, and were not prepared. I do not know these people, so I go to help Will.

I say, "So, they're back at last!" because although it is a silly comment to make, I do not know what else to say.

Will does not answer at once. He has a strange look on his face, sort of stressed, and although he says, "It's good, isn't it?" the colours of his words are dark and bleak.

Just then the tall man comes over and reaches across the counter where Will and I are preparing to serve drinks. The man is still holding Gracie, who has her thumb in her mouth, but he has a spare arm. He puts his hand on Will's head and says, "Son, I am more proud of you than I can possibly say."

Then Will stops still, with a teaspoon full of coffee halfway to a cup, and seems to sort of freeze. Then he drops the spoon with a little clatter and bursts into tears.

In no time the man is round our side of the counter. He holds Will up close against him and pats and strokes his hair, and says, "My son! My son!"

I get out of the way. Someone, one of the returnees, says to me, "Hi, I'm Madge." It is an old lady, and I know I should be polite, but I am watching Will and his dad, and Gracie in their dad's arms, then Pixie having her hair stroked by her mum, and I feel a big, empty feeling, like a hollow inside me. So I just say, "Hi!" to the old woman and then rush out through the kitchen door and across to the children's room. I sit upstairs on the sleeping bags and I cry, and I think that I will never have a mum or a dad, and I wonder what will happen to me.

Much later, Vishna comes across to find me. She says, "They're going to have a Meeting for worship now, for Thanksgiving. Do you want to come?"

But I say, "I just want to go home." So we leave the city and climb the Hill, and I do not want a snack. I lie on my sleeping bag and feel cold, and I think that there is nobody in this world that I really belong to and nobody to say they are proud of me, and I wish I had not lost my parents, and I wish my parents had not been Quakers who got themselves disappeared and left me behind to be Scum of the Earth.

★ ★ ★

After that I will not go to the Quaker Meeting anymore. Vishna still goes, every Sunday morning. While she is away, I sit in our shelter and feel angry. The Old Man asks me, "Do we need to have a talk, Giorgio?" but I just say, rather rudely, "No, we don't." When Vishna says, "Will says hi," I do not answer. When she says, "They're fixing up the Meeting House; it looks quite different now," I say, "Who cares?" I am more or less all right if we keep away from the subject of the Quakers, and we do some good after-Christmas gleaning and have a feast of ready-meals which are only just past their sell-by dates, and which are supposed to go in a microwave but taste really good the way Vishna cooks them. Despite that, though, I am unhappy all the time. It feels as if I have eaten a stone and it has got stuck in my tummy.

Then one day I am sitting by our fire feeling angry, and Vishna has gone to the Quaker Meeting, and I am feeling annoyed with the rain, and the cold, and the mud, and with Skye because she has not been back for ages, and with the Old Man because he looks at me with that concerned expression, and generally I am angry with the whole world. Then I hear voices, and it is people coming closer, talking to each other, and one of them is Vishna, and the other one is Will.

When they arrive at the fireside Vishna says, stating the obvious, "I've brought us a visitor."

I do not look at Will. I say grumpily to Vishna, "It's not safe to bring visitors here. Now we'll have to move."

Vishna says, "Giorgi…" Then she stops. She says to Will, "So anyway, this is where we live. I won't be a minute…" and she goes off up to the copse where the big fire ring is, as if she has something important to do, although I'm sure she has not.

Will sits down on the log opposite mine. He says, "Wow! This is cool! I can't imagine living like this, all the year round. It's like an adventure."

I do not look at Will. I poke the fire and I say, "It isn't an adventure to be Scum of the Earth, and feckless, and to have no mum and dad. It's just cold and wet and muddy." And then I think a bit more, and I say the thing that has been nearly in my mouth to say ever since the Sunday after Christmas when the Quaker grown-ups came back. "It's lonely."

And then I start to cry.

Perhaps Little Bear would have known what to do if I had cried, but back when the big camp was here I did not have much cause for crying, and anyhow there were always grown-ups around to pick us up and patch us up in those days. Perhaps it is because he has two sisters, but Will knows just what to do so that I do not feel stupid and I do not feel I ought to get a grip. He moves across and sits on my log, next to me, which is quite a tight squeeze, but friendly too. He puts an arm round my back and for a bit he does not say anything, not a word.

So there we are, me all hunched over and crying, and Will with his arm round me, and the wind blowing and little flurries of rain falling on us.

Finally Will says, very kindly, "Giorgio, would you mind crying inside, because it's beginning to rain quite hard!"

Then suddenly it seems funny, and I do not exactly stop crying but it turns itself into laughing without me doing anything, and I say, "Oh! I'm sorry!" and we go into the shelter out of the wet, and we are both almost laughing.

Will says, "It must have been tough for you, when all the parents came back and you still don't have yours."

I say, "It's silly of me, really." Then I think it really *is* silly of me. I say, "I don't remember them at all. I can't be missing people I would not recognise if I saw them in the street, can I? And I've got Vishna and Skye, and the Old Man. I think they all love me."

Will says, "Vishna told me about Skye. She's like your adopted mum, isn't she? Who's the Old Man?"

So then I explain, and we talk about the camp which used to be here, and Will tells me about moving back into their proper house now that their parents have returned, and about not telling the teachers in his school about why they were away for so long because nobody wants the school to be suspicious about whether Will's family are good citizens. And after a while Vishna comes back and says to me, "I promised Will a snack," and I say quite cheerfully, "Let's make dampers," and the stone has gone from my tummy. Then Will asks, "Do you have a silence before you eat?" and Vishna says, "That's a good idea," and as we sit by the fire for a few seconds of silence the pink colour of *welcome* comes into my mind, and I know that next Sunday I will go to the Quaker Meeting again because, as Vishna said, I sort of belong there.

★ ★ ★

When Skye comes back, a couple of evenings later, she finds Vishna and me sitting by our fire talking about *Swallows and Amazons*. We have been trying to read it together, sometimes with me reading aloud and sometimes Vishna, but really it is the wrong time of year for reading books. We have had several quite dark days and they have been cool too, so we have needed to be on the move. If we were not feckless, and lived in a house like Will, we would have electricity. Will has told me that he and Pixie read to themselves every evening before they go to sleep, reading from proper books, not droids, because Will's mum says it is best to be screen-free for an hour at least before sleep. Gracie cannot read very well yet, although Will says she pretends she can, so their mum or dad read her a short story each evening. "Sometimes," Will says, "if Gracie can't go to sleep, they sing songs to her."

I ask, "What do they sing?" and my heart gives a sort of thump, but Will says, "Oh, you know. Kids' stuff. Like 'Hush Little Baby, Don't You Cry' or 'Sleep, Little Baby, Sleep'." I have never heard of these songs, and I am disappointed, but I am glad to know that Quaker parents sing to their children, because I hope that I started to learn *Bed is too small for my tired head* and *How can I keep from singing?* in the same way.

Anyhow, as we do not have electricity, and it is too dark to read aloud, Vishna and I have started making up a sort of alternative story, which we have called *Robins and Blackbirds*. Each night, when we are in our sleeping bags, one of us has to make up the next chapter, taking over from where we left off the night before. In our story there are four Robins: Will, Pixie, Vishna and me. The Blackbirds do not yet have names. When Skye arrives we are trying to think what they might be called, and making up more and more silly names, and laughing very hard.

Skye says, "Now, that is a sound I love to hear!" and she opens the door to the Professor's shelter, which now has the plaque I made for Skye for Christmas hanging on the post in front. She dumps her backpack just inside and asks, "I don't suppose you've got any water on the boil, have you?" which is another way of saying, *I'm dying for a cup of tea!* So we all drink tea, and we tell Skye about trying to find names for the Blackbirds, and she says that they should be called Fred, Bert and Bill, and we all laugh because the names are so old-fashioned.

Then, of course, Skye has news to tell us, and she wants to know what we have been doing. I tell her that long trousers are all very well but that they easily get muddy on the Hill, and then, if I wash them, they are impossible to get dry at this time of the year. And I tell her that Will sometimes wears shorts, even in the winter.

Skye says, looking at Vishna, not at me, "So, you're still going to Meeting, then?"

Vishna glances sideways at me. She does not want to say anything I might not want Skye to know. Then she says, "I have been. Giorgi has been taking a short break."

But I want to tell Skye the truth. I say, "I felt sad and angry when Will's mum and dad came back, and I still haven't found mine. It doesn't seem fair."

Skye says, "Oh, Giorgi..." but of course there is nothing else to say after that.

Vishna says, helping me, "But you're working on that, aren't you, Giorgi?" and I feel grateful to her, because *working on that* could mean a lot of different things, and I cannot explain to Skye what I do not quite understand myself.

Skye says, "Well, we are nearly over the worst of the winter now," and I am not sure what her words have got to do with what we have been talking about. I think she really means, "Okay, Giorgi, we don't need to talk about your mum and dad if you aren't ready." Then she says, "Let me tell you about Little Bear, and all the family." So we hear about Walking Tall bringing them all to Edinburgh for Hogmanay, and Little Bear wearing a jacket exactly like mine, and Big Bear finding a girlfriend who has lived on Shetland all her life, and how they keep chickens but so far they have not laid any eggs, and how Little Bear's mum has been given a recipe for the best fruit cake in the world, and how they had all seen the Swedish journalist's article and Little Bear had given a talk to his class about when he used to live on the Hill, and how Little Bear has already got a Scottish accent. And I think that one day, when I have found my mum and dad, I will go to Scotland too, because I really miss Little Bear.

Then Skye tells us that she has really only popped in for one night, to check on us and to have a word with the Old Man, and tomorrow she needs to be somewhere else by midday so it will mean another early start. Then she goes across to the Old Man's shelter for her word, and I say to Vishna, "Thank you," because she saved me from having to explain. And Vishna just says, "You're welcome," not, *Thank you for what?* and that shows how much Vishna always seems to understands about what is going on.

★ ★ ★

It actually feels good to be going to the Quaker Meeting again. I wake up early, when it is still quite dark. The afternoons always start to lighten up before the mornings, of course. We are long past the shortest day now. That was before Christmas, before Will's parents came home. I lie in bed listening to our wind chimes making a woody *clonk, click, hum* outside the shelter, and a noise which is probably the Old Man moving around in his shelter. You can hear things quite differently with your ear right down on the ground. I think that I am going to sit in silence, and I wonder whether I will see the colours today. I wonder whether anyone will stand up and talk, and whether it will be the Goodness helping me along my way. I wonder whether Will will remember to bring a torch, so that Vishna and I can read *Swallows and Amazons* before we go to sleep. I wonder whether anyone will have made muffins. I am ready to go before Vishna has even plaited her hair, and I feel like running down the Hill, although that is not wise if you want to keep your long jeans free of mud.

There is no lookout in the road. Instead, someone I do not know is standing at the open gate, shaking hands with people as they arrive. Vishna says, "The Quakers are not a banned organisation. Once that article was published and the Canadians and Europeans started asking awkward questions, they had to ease up." Then she says, "Hello!" to the shaking-hands woman, who says, "Hello, Vishna, hello there!" in return. Vishna adds to me, talking a little over her shoulder because I am behind her, "A reporter from *Around Europe* was here a couple of weeks ago, standing in the street taking photos. Winchester Meeting is a little bit famous!"

Then we go inside.

The large meeting room feels quite different. They have mended the broken window so it is not boarded up anymore. Someone has taken all the newspaper off the other window. I do not know whether the electricity had been cut off, before, or whether they just avoided using the lights because they did not want to attract attention. Anyhow, now the lights on the walls are on. Instead of a candle on the table someone has put some holly twigs with red berries in a jug, and there are books arranged around the leaves. There are two circles of chairs instead of one, an inside and an outside circle, and for a moment it feels like a different place, and I do not know where to sit. Then I see Will in a corner by the window and he gives a little sign, which means *Sit here!* So I go and join him, and it feels like my Meeting again.

It is different, though. There are more people, and Will or Pixie are not in charge anymore. It makes them seem younger. Gracie is not in the room at all. It takes me a long time to settle down, although I see that Vishna is engrossed in the silence almost at once. She is sitting sideways on to Will and me, and it is the first time I notice how beautiful she is.

Several of the grown-ups talk. Their words have colours, but they are the ordinary colours that words usually have.

The silence in between is plain, but I do not mind. I have a content feeling. I am thinking that I know a beautiful person who is like a sister, and I have a friend I am sitting next to, and Skye pops in, even just for one night, to check up on us, and the Old Man is always there. Then the golden light of the Goodness shines gently and I nearly feel like crying, but I do not. So I sing in my heart the words, *Yet what can I give him? Give my heart.*

★ ★ ★

Then, during the notices after the Meeting, Percy says that there will be a Meeting in the home of Will's mum and dad. It will be on the following evening, and everyone is welcome to a bring-and-share supper. I do not know what that is, but Vishna does. They held one a few weeks earlier to welcome all the grown-ups back from prison. This one is so that we can all be given more information about the national picture, and one or two of the adults want to talk about their experiences of being locked up. Some people from other Meetings in the area might come too.

I say to Vishna, who is drinking hot water and eating an ordinary biscuit (no muffins today), "What did you take to the last bring-and-share?"

She says, "I didn't take anything. I didn't go. I couldn't see how I would get there, and anyhow, all our food except our fruit and veg is past its sell-by date, and I didn't think I could just take some carrots!"

Will overhears. He says, "You can come, even if you don't bring any food. There's always too much."

When he has turned to talk to the old lady, Madge, Vishna says, "We can't go, Will. I don't like the idea of sponging off the Quakers, and anyhow, how would we get there? It's a really long walk from the Hill to Harestock."

I see that this is true. Harestock is on the other edge of the city, past the hospital and the old prison, past the houses and school they built around the time of the New Alliance, and past the big, private hospital which the Americans and the rich people use. It would take at least an hour to walk there, and it would look odd. The police might stop us to find out why we were out and about in the evening, and want to see our IDs, and I would end up in care. All to go to one bring-and-share supper.

Then Will's mum comes over and says to Vishna, "I hope you will come tomorrow evening?"

Vishna looks embarrassed. She says, "I don't think we can, but thank you for inviting us."

Then Pixie joins the group. Of course, Pixie has known all along who we are and where we live, because she was the one driving the van, when she came to the bottom of the Hill to tell us that the People had been arrested. She has heard what her mum has said to us, and Vishna's reply. She says, "Mum, they can't come. They live on St Catherine's Hill. How would they get there?"

Then her mum looks embarrassed, and says, "Oh, my goodness! Yes, of course... Let me talk to Ted." And a few minutes later it is agreed that someone will give us a lift, if we wait at the parking space where the People used to bring us food and water.

★ ★ ★

We tell the Old Man, of course. He does not say much, but he smiles a slow smile. His only comment is, "You are becoming quite respectable, going to supper in a house in Harestock!"

Vishna says, "A *Quaker* house!"

And the Old Man says, "You have a point!", because

although the Quakers are not feckless they are certainly not very respectable!

Vishna and I are waiting at the car park a bit before the cathedral clock strikes six thirty, in the trees where we cannot easily be spotted. It is dark and cold, with hard rain in the wind, which is nearly sleet. We do not have to wait long. A car drives along and stops, and Will jumps out of the front passenger seat. When he opens the door a light inside the car comes on, and I can see Will's mum. Will says, "Giorgio! Vishna! Are you here?"

We come out from our hiding place, and Will gives a sort of hop of excitement. He opens a back door of the car, and Vishna climbs in. She was used to cars before she became feckless. I follow her. As far as I can remember this is my first time in any vehicle, and as soon as the door is closed I feel a scary, shut-in feeling.

Vishna's mum says, "Hi, you two! Seat belts, please!"

Vishna reaches out and buckles up at once, but I do not know what to do. I cannot see a seat belt on my side. Vishna realises my predicament and says, "Here," and reaches across and finds a strap lying flat against the seat. When she tugs it, it comes out almost as if it is on elastic, and she finds a clip and fixes it in. Then I feel even more trapped.

Vishna says, by way of making conversation, "Nice car!"

Will says, "It's our only car. We used to have two, but we gave one up. For environmental reasons. You don't have a car at all, do you?"

I think that is a very silly thing to say, given that Will knows perfectly well that we are Scum of the Earth and only own the clothes on our backs. After all, he has visited our camp. So I say, "I have never even been in a car before."

We are driving along one of the back roads into the city now. I feel as if we are going very fast, although the notices tell us there is a twenty-mile-per-hour speed limit. Will says, "Wow!" and I think he does not know what to say.

Vishna says, "Giorgi has lived on the Hill for most of his life."

Will's mother says, "Yes, of course. It's easy to forget…"

We very quickly reach the middle part of the town, where many of the shops still have bright lights shining on their window displays, giving the darkness a sort of strange magic. We can see down the precinct where only delivery vehicles can go, and then only before nine in the morning. There are people walking about. Since the shops are closed I know they will be going to the restaurants and the pubs. I think, *There could be some good gleaning tomorrow morning.*

Then Will's mum makes the car go up the Romsey Road, and we just about fly past the old prison, all lit up with lights on the walls to stop people escaping, and the old hospital, and then the newer houses and the smart private hospital which says it has been given five stars. I am looking out of the side window of the car, not saying anything, but holding on very tight to the armrest, because I feel that if we were to crash I would not stand a chance, going this fast. There are no people walking along the pavement. A police car drives towards us and I hold my breath, because if they stop us and ask for our papers I am done for, but Will's mum just raises her hand, as if she knows the officers, and we do not even slow down.

Then we get to a roundabout, take a turn and then another turn, and pull into a driveway. There is a big house in front of us, with a garden at the front, and some trees, and there are lots of lights, and other cars parked up and down the road. I feel like a person in a storybook.

Will jumps out, and says, "Come on, Giorgi, I want to show you my room!"

But I just stand by the car and look up at the house, and my mouth goes dry, and I do not want to go in.

Vishna asks me quietly, "What's up?"

I say, "If the police come, we will be trapped in there."

Vishna says, "The police won't come, Giorgi." Then she sees how frightened I am. She says, "It's no different from going into the library, or the milk bar, or the shops."

I say, "But is there another exit?" I am thinking that if the police come in through the front door, which Will's mum has opened, and from which a stream of yellow light is shining into the darkness, we could all be trapped.

Vishna laughs, although not as if I have said anything funny. She says, "Yes, there will be a door out through the kitchen, and probably glass doors from the living room into the garden."

So then I feel better, and we go in, and Pixie says I may hang my jacket up, but I think I would prefer to keep it with me, in case we need to make a quick getaway. Vishna goes into the room called the living room, where lots of the Quakers are already sitting in groups, talking, and I check in the kitchen, so that I have seen at least one other way out, before Will takes me up to his room.

Will's bedroom is bigger than the shelter which Vishna and I share. In fact, it is bigger than our shelter and the Professor's (which is now Skye's) combined. There is a bed, high up, with a ladder going up to it, and underneath there is a desk with a blue droid like the ones in the library. On the wall there is another screen, and I see at least two other droids lying on a shelf. I say to Will, "Wow! You must be really rich!"

Will says, "Not really rich, but comfortable."

I go over to his bookshelf and look at the row of interesting books. "These are the ones you read before you go to sleep?" I ask. Walking across Will's bedroom is like walking on blue moss, because it is soft and springy underfoot. Everything is very clean, with no mud at all on anything, and I feel dirty. The air is warm, like summer, and there is a smell I do not recognise. Will says, "I wanted to show you this," and he gives me a photograph to look at, in a frame. It shows a group of kids in summer clothes standing by the little wooden hut which is the children's room at the Quaker Meeting House. "This is all of us, last summer, before the arrests," he says. I see Will and Pixie standing with the two who are obviously the twins, and I see Gracie, holding a doll, sitting cross-legged by a little boy in dungarees. It reminds me of the way we were last summer, before the others went north.

Then Will's mum calls up the stairs, "Kids! We're about to eat," and we go down again and into the brightly lit living room, where there is a lot of food displayed on plates on a table, and some of the Quakers already have drinks in glasses. Will's dad suggests, "Shall we have a short silence, to give thanks?" and everyone stops talking, but I am not giving thanks. I cannot concentrate. I am thinking about the richness of the house, and that I am not as clean as I thought I was, and about how warm the air is, and about whether there are glass doors out into the garden, by which we could escape if the police come, behind the red floor-to-ceiling curtains at the far end of the room.

Skye was always very strict with me about my table manners, even though we have never had a table. I remember the Professor saying once, to Skye, "It's good to see that you haven't let your standards drop." Tonight I am pleased Skye held up our standards. I know to keep my mouth closed when I chew, and not to talk when my mouth is full of food, and not to take huge bites even though some of the cakes are so delicious, and not to lick my knife. I am not quite sure about the coloured squares of paper, but I see people patting their mouths with them, and wiping their fingers, and I use my red square in the same way, and when I have finished I screw it up and leave it on my plate, just the way other people do. I think that my fingers still feel a bit sticky, though, and I know that I would feel a bit more comfortable if there was a tuft or two of wet grass nearby, to get rid of the sugar.

And then Percy says, "Well, Friends. Shall we get down to the real business of the evening?" and people on chairs cross their legs or rearrange the cushions, and shuffle in their seats. Will, Pixie and I are sitting on the floor, on a patterned rug, opposite the armchair where Will's dad is sitting. His mum perches on the arm of the chair, and his dad puts an arm round her, and it reminds me of Walking Tall and Little Bear's mum, making friends again after they'd had that row about going north. I have seen so many new things that when we have a silence to settle our spirits, my mind remains unsettled.

Until they start to talk.

★ ★ ★

Percy says, "I'll kick off," as if we are going to play football. He is giving us the background, putting what has happened to the Winchester Quakers in context. He reminds us that Quakers have always, right from the start, found it difficult to be very cooperative with governments. He says, "Of course, we all know about Quaker businesses which were started because the professions were barred to us, and we never forget the conscientious objectors of World War I." Then he reminds everyone that once again the universities are difficult to access because a lot of Quakers will not swear the new Oath of Allegiance, and that it is becoming usual for people once again to start their own business and to be self-employed. These are things I do not understand, but Will nudges me and says in a whisper, "Like my dad."

Percy says that the Quakers were not happy with a thing called *austerity* even before England left the European Union (which happened a long time ago, I know, before I was born). He says that way back, right from the start, Winchester Quakers were concerned about homelessness, and that their first big run-in with the authorities happened a while ago. "For the last ten or twelve years," says Percy, "we have run the risk of arrests and disappearances, but until now the authorities have always targeted individuals. We have never been a banned organisation."

A few people nod and make grunts of agreement. Some look sad, and I wonder if they knew the people who disappeared. I remember that Skye's friend was a Quaker, and she disappeared too. I wonder where they go, and then I think that they are probably doing Hard Labour somewhere, or in prison in Cuba or Puerto Rico.

Percy says, "So the mass arrest in the autumn was totally unexpected. We are the only Meeting so far to have suffered this sort of persecution, and fortunately our story became internationally known, which is why we are all able to meet freely again now."

One man says, "I don't think we should take our freedom for granted."

And a woman says, "I think the York Quakers are experiencing quite a lot of difficulty."

Percy nods. "Yes," he agrees. "You're both right. And the American Friends are having a pretty tough time too. But just now, following the international outcry, there is likely to be a period of easing up."

Will's father says, "And our imprisonment was not without its benefits."

"Exactly," says Percy. "And that is why we have called this Meeting."

I whisper to Will, "Have you heard all this before?" After all, he is living in a house with two people who were in prison.

Will whispers back, "Sort of."

Percy goes on, "So, at this point, I'd like to ask Jenny to tell us what happened."

Jenny is quite a young woman. She is wearing a loose,

colourful dress and I see that she is pregnant. She says, "Well, you probably all know that we were sitting in Meeting for Worship." People nod again and look interested. She says, "Actually, I was about to go out. I was feeling a bit sick. Then a group of the anti-terrorists came bursting in through the gate and into the meeting room."

"They had guns!" says another woman.

"Yes," agrees Jenny. "It was quite frightening. And they wouldn't let us talk."

Will's dad says, "I asked them by what right they had disturbed a lawfully constituted act of Christian worship."

Several people smile.

Jenny says, "Yes, and it made them even more angry. They said '*Christian* worship?' as if they thought we belonged to some quite different religion, and one of them said, 'A bunch of troublemakers'!"

"Well, we are!" whispers Will, and Pixie giggles on the other side of me.

Jenny continues, "So, they took us out to the street, and there was a large black bus there…"

"With the windows covered," says someone else, "and they brought the children from the crèche."

"And we were thinking of the older ones, doing a nature trail…"

"Then they drove us away," finishes Jenny.

We are all quiet. Without planning to, I ask, "Where did they take you? To a labour camp?"

Lots of people look at me, and smile. Percy says, "Well, now we get to the interesting part."

Will's mother says, "They took us to the old prison, on the Romsey Road."

Will's father says, "And they put us all in this one, large room…"

"It was the chapel," says Will's mum.

213

"Did they separate you?" asks Vishna. She is sitting on a settee between two older ladies.

"No," say several people, more or less at the same time.

Will's dad says, "I got the feeling that they didn't really know what to do with us."

His mum says, "I overheard one of the anti-terrorists arguing with a prison officer. The officer was saying that this was a prison, not a detention centre, and that the anti-terrorists had no right to bring big groups of people there."

Percy says, "Well, of course, there's no love lost between the old law enforcement agencies and the anti-terrorists."

"So they just left us there," says Jenny.

Will's mum says, "We can't complain about the way the prison officers treated us."

There are nods of agreement. Jenny says, "They brought us food, and there are bathrooms by the chapel. But it was worrying because we didn't know what was happening. And we didn't know where the older kids were."

"You were gone for weeks," says Vishna. "Were you in the chapel all that time?"

Will's dad says, "We kept a record of the days, marking them off on the wall."

His mum says, "We were not the first ones to do that, either!"

Jenny says, "Then the Bishop of Winchester came, and we heard about the Swedish newspaper article, and they gave us cells but they didn't lock them, so we could visit each other up and down the wing but we couldn't get out."

"And *that*," says Will's mum, "is when the exciting bit happened."

Everyone is quiet. For a few seconds all you can hear in the room is the hum of something electrical in the kitchen. Then Will's dad says, "We discovered that we were not the first Quakers to be housed in Winchester prison."

Will's mum says, "Well, of course, we knew there had been

conscientious objectors there, during the First World War, but we discovered that there had been other Friends there, more recently."

Jenny says, "We even found things they had scratched on the walls, in the paintwork!"

Someone asks, almost breathlessly, "What things?"

"Names and dates," says Jenny. "Not World War I names and dates, but the names and dates of people we knew, or have heard of. People who disappeared, from this Meeting!"

"And a song," says Will's mum. "We found the words of a song, scratched in the paintwork behind a mattress, where a bunk was up against the wall."

"It was a song some of us knew," says Will's dad. "So we taught everyone else."

"And we sang it," says Jenny, "every day."

"What was the song?" I ask, and that tight feeling is in my chest again, as if I cannot breathe.

"We are going to sing it to you now," says Will's mum. "All of us who were in prison."

Then Jenny hums a note and they start to sing, a song which is both sad and happy:

My life flows on in endless song,
Above earth's lamentation,
I hear the sweet, though far-off hymn,
That hails a new creation.

Through all the tumult and the strife
I hear the music ringing.
It finds an echo in my soul –
How can I keep from singing?

What though my joys and comforts die,
The Lord my saviour liveth.

What though the darkness gathers round,
Songs in the night he giveth.

I lift my eyes, the cloud grows dim,
I see the blue above it.
And day by day this pathway smooths,
Since first I learnt to love it.

We have no home, no freedom here,
To temporal hopes no clinging.
And yet we know the light of Truth,
How can we keep from singing?

So here we languish, not alone,
A well of joy is springing,
For love and truth and light will reign,
How can we keep from singing?

Some of the Quakers are singing with their eyes closed, others are looking upwards. The song is sad and joyful, full of peace and a sort of kindness, like being hugged. They do not see that I am crying until the last note is sung and we are all in silence. Then Vishna looks across the room at me and says, "What's the matter, Giorgi?"

And I look at her, and I say, my voice coming out all croaky, "That is the song my parents used to sing to me. Before I lost them. They sang me that song."

And everyone is very quiet. Then the old lady, Madge, says, "Giorgi? Are you Giorgio Green, the son of Filippo and Annie?"

Then everyone is talking, and Vishna is hugging me, and some other people are crying too, and there is a lump the size of an apple in my throat, and I wish Skye were there, or Little Bear, and I think, *This is who I am. I am Giorgio Green. I am the son of Filippo and Annie Green.* And it does not seem real at all.

Epilogue

The little cottage where I live with Little Bear and all his family is made of stone and painted white on the outside. We are still living on a hill, but this time we look out towards the sea and across at another island. At one time the cottage just had two rooms, but it has been extended now, so that there are three bedrooms, a bathroom, a kitchen and a living room. We have no stairs, like there were in Will's house, but we have heating so that the air feels warm when you come in from outside, after school or if you have been helping Walking Tall on the smallholding.

At first I thought the cottage was very big, but now that I have been to play at the MacDonalds' house along the road, I realise that it is really just average for this island. The MacDonalds' house is made of wood and painted dark red, and it has a huge picture window in the living room, which also looks out over the sea. Mr MacDonald made a lot of money out of oil, when it was big, although he moved to renewables a while ago because, he says, he saw the writing on the wall.

Compared with the rooms in the MacDonalds' house, our rooms are small, and Little Bear and I sleep on bunk beds. We both wanted to sleep on the top bunk, and Little Bear's mum said we had to settle our differences before we drove her mad, so now we take it turn and turn about, switching over each time the sheets are changed. I found it very difficult, at first, to have a duvet instead of a sleeping bag. Every night it slipped off me, and I would wake up in the morning freezing cold. Little Bear used to say, "I don't know what your problem is!" and throw his pillow at me. Then quite suddenly, without me doing anything, the duvet stopped slipping off, and now I wake up with it tucked around my shoulders, and I am snug and warm.

Little Bear's mum has let us put up posters and pictures on the wall. Little Bear supports a football team in Aberdeen, so we have soccer pictures up, and I have put up a copy of the Swedish journalist's article, and an old photograph of Filippo and Annie Green, who are the parents I lost. The Swedish journalist tried to trace them for me, but the English government denies that they were ever arrested, or that anyone ever disappears, so maybe I have lost them for good. But the Winchester Quakers had this photograph, and I see that Filippo, my dad, was Italian-looking and Annie, my mum, was English. Some of the Quakers still remember them. They told me they were good people.

At school I have two names on the register: Giorgio Green. I am proud of them both. We do not have to carry identity cards, although if I ever want to visit Vishna, who is studying art in Dublin, I will have to have a proper passport, and that will say *Giorgio Green* too.

There is a little group of Quakers here. They know my story, because the Swedish journalist made a big thing of it. We only meet once a month, and on the other Sundays all our family works on the smallholding and we have a roast dinner in the evening. And I think it is true, those words which my mum and dad used to sing to me. Except very occasionally, like when I have toothache, I really cannot keep from singing.